Agatha Christie's

A Murder
is Announced

Adapted for the stage by
Leslie Darbon

Samuel French - London
New York - Toronto - Hollywood

A MURDER IS ANNOUNCED

First presented by Peter Saunders at the Theatre Royal, Brighton; and subsequently at the Vaudeville Theatre, London, on September 21st, 1977, with the following cast of characters:

CHARACTERS

Julia Simmons	Patricia Brake
Letitia Blacklock	Dinah Sheridan
Dora Bunner	Eleanor Summerfield
Patrick Simmons	Christopher Scoular
Mitzi	Mia Nadasi
Miss Marple	Dulcie Gray
Phillipa Haymes	Barbara Flynn
Mrs Swettenham	Nancy Nevinson
Edmund Swettenham	Gareth Armstrong
Rudi Scherz	Michael Dyerball
Inspector Craddock	James Grout
Sergeant Mellors	Michael Fleming

The play directed by Robert Chetwyn
Setting by Anthony Holland

The action takes place in two drawing-rooms in an early Victorian house in Chipping Cleghorn which have been made into one room

ACT I Scene 1 The morning of Friday the 13th
   Scene 2 6.10 p.m. the same day
   Scene 3 The following Saturday morning

ACT II Scene 1 The following Sunday afternoon
   Scene 2 The following Monday morning
   Scene 3 6 p.m. the same day

Time—Agatha Christie time

ACT I

SCENE 1

Two drawing-rooms in an early Victorian house in Chipping Cleghorn which have been made into one room. The morning of Friday the thirteenth The wall which originally separated the two rooms was clearly a bearer-wall since part of it has had to be left intact. This is upstage and has a door almost directly next to it. This door is kept locked and will be referred to as the Locked Door. In front of the remaining piece of wall—which juts out into the room—there is an occasional table of some quality. It is a real crafts-man's piece with fine cabriole legs, beautifully carved. It is placed in this position in an attempt to help "integrate" the two rooms more. On this table there is a Dresden lamp. A shepherdess. A quality piece of porcelain. Beside it is a silver cigarette-box which is kept highly polished. Beside the "jutting out" piece of wall L, is a Sheraton bureau—without doubt a delight to live with. On top of this is an exquisite Art Nouveau china vase. Something very distinctive. Further along L, we come to the Main Door. A very wide door since it was fashioned in the days when ladies wore crinolines and the width made it easier for them to pass through into the room. In the L wall is a large fireplace with a carved surround—well in keeping with the general surround-ings. On the mantelpiece we find a magnificent clock. French in origin—Empire period—of a predominantly squarish shape but with beautiful ornamental brasswork. It has the most exquisite chime. To one side of the fireplace there is a sideboard which contains drinks and glasses, etc. It is heavy and not quite the same taste as the other pieces of furniture—but, it is practical

In what was the smaller of the two drawing-rooms, R, there is a bay window. It reaches from floor to ceiling as was the custom in all houses during the period this one was built. It has rich velvet and net curtains. In the bay is a sofa. The walls are festooned with paintings. Not especially good, since most of them are family portraits. There are also a few late eighteenth- early nineteenth-century silhouettes, which were done when the family were not so well off as they had been. In a further attempt to disguise the fact that it was originally two rooms, the chairs are set in a semicircle. Most people will not be conscious of this and, of course, this is what was hoped for. There are quite a few interesting and comfortable chairs. Two spoon-backs. One grand-mother and one grandfather. An upright "throne" chair. A low tub-shape. A fat comfortable looking button-back; and so on. In the middle of the cleverly placed semicircle there is a small centre table of good shape and nicely proportioned. It is not a big table and can easily be lifted by one person. There is a central light—probably a chandelier—and some wall lights

The whole effect is of simple elegance. Not something merely to look at although pleasing to the eye—it is something to be lived in

As the Curtain rises, Miss Blacklock is at the bay window waving good-bye to someone. She is beyond middle-age, but still a very attractive woman who has clearly looked after her figure and features. Julia Simmons, her niece, aged twenty-five or twenty-six, is sitting in a chair reading a newspaper

Miss Blacklock Good-bye.
Julia You really do make too much fuss of her, Aunt Letty . . .

Miss Blacklock turns from the window and moves to Julia—a small smile on her face

Miss Blacklock Well, Phillipa's been through rather a lot, Julia. And tell me what's wrong with trying to make life a bit more pleasant?
Julia Nothing—I suppose . . .
Miss Blacklock It's such a little thing—waving good-bye. But, it helps. I'd do the same for you.
Julia I'm family!

Miss Blacklock picks up a newspaper and sits in a chair

Miss Blacklock (*chuckling*) Why, Julia. It sounds as if you're jealous.
Julia Me? Certainly not! But, she is only a lodger.
Miss Blacklock Come to that. So are you.

A moment passes. Julia appears a little hurt

Look. I was pleased to have you here—and just as pleased to have Phillipa. She's had a lot to contend with. How would you feel if your husband had died so young leaving you with a child . . .
Julia I don't know. *I* wouldn't have got married in my teens. I'm not so daft.
Miss Blacklock Ah—the trouble is, we're not all as worldly as you are, Julia.

A moment's pause as Miss Blacklock's point registers

Julia I'm sorry, Aunt Letty . . .
Miss Blacklock Oh—there's no need . . .
Julia No, no—I've been spiteful. And, believe it or not, I rather like Phillipa. We seem to be on the same wave length. But, you do make too much fuss—of all of us.
Miss Blacklock I like having young people around me. So when your mother asked if you could stay here, I was delighted. It meant I could indulge myself . . .

The Main Door opens and Dora Bunner enters. She is slightly older than Miss Blacklock

Bunny I can't find it, Letty. I can't find it *anywhere*.

Miss Blacklock looks up from her newspaper and smiles benignly

Miss Blacklock What dear?

Bunny goes to her

Bunny It's Friday . . .

Miss Blacklock (*with a wry smile*) All day, dear.

Bunny Yes.

Julia Friday, the thirteenth to be precise. *Ominous!*

Bunny (*worried*) Oh, dear . . . What was I saying, Letty?

Miss Blacklock You couldn't find *it*, Bunny dear.

Bunny Exactly. I can't find it anywhere. Have you seen it?

Miss Blacklock (*smiling*) Let's start at the beginning.

Bunny It's Friday—I always read it Friday morning after breakfast . . .

Miss Blacklock Oh, the *Gazette*, you mean . . .

Bunny Of course. That's what I've been telling you . . .

Miss Blacklock Yes, dear . . .

Bunny I can't find the *Chipping Cleghorn Gazette* anywhere. (*With a sudden thought*) You don't think they've gone on strike, do you?

Miss Blacklock They wouldn't do that, dear. Not *here*.

Julia What a lovely thought. A strike. Here. *Picket lines*—headlines in the national press . . . We might even be on the wireless. "Reporters on *Chipping Cleghorn Gazette* refuse to report Vicar's garden party".

Miss Blacklock Things like that don't happen here . . .

Julia No. *Nothing* happens here. It's another world, isn't it?

Miss Blacklock And just as well, too.

Patrick Simmons, Julia's brother enters through the Main Door, reading the Chipping Cleghorn Gazette. *He is a year older than his sister; a very handsome young man. He chuckles as he reads*

Patrick Listen to this. It's marvellous. Abso-blooming-lutely marvellous.

Julia (*sarcastically*) Oh, Patrick—*do* tell us what it is. We're all dying to know.

Patrick Oh, dear. We are in a bad mood, aren't we? Have a bad dream last night?

Julia A nightmare. It was all about you.

Patrick Well—it's better than being ignored . . .

Miss Blacklock What's so marvellous, Patrick?

Patrick The Personal Column in this rag, Aunt Letty. It's better than Evelyn Home. Listen to this. (*Reading*) "Young woman, said to be excitingly beautiful, seeks companionship with mature man. Love. Marriage. Rolls-Royce owners only." (*He looks at Bunny*) Really, Bunny. I'm surprised at you. Wouldn't a Bentley owner be just as suitable?

Miss Blacklock (*to Patrick*) You know very well, young man, that Bunny *always* reads the *Gazette* first. I don't have many rules in this house but that's one. She's been looking everywhere for it.

Patrick Well—she could have borrowed Mitzi's.

Julia Mitzi?

Patrick She thinks it will help her to speak English.

Bunny comes back to life again at the mention of Mitzi

Bunny Oh, dear me, no. I couldn't—I really couldn't. I've only got to walk past the kitchen and she snarls at me. I only want to help—that's all. I couldn't ask her—I just couldn't. She's horrid, that Millie.
Miss Blacklock Mitzi, dear.
Bunny Yes.
Miss Blacklock Well, you won't have to ask her, Bunny.
Patrick It's all yours, Bunny. (*He gives her the newspaper*)
Bunny Thank you, Patrick.
Patrick And I promise I won't borrow it again.
Bunny (*coldly*) Why aren't you at College? It wouldn't have happened if you'd been at College . . .
Patrick I haven't got a lecture till this afternoon.
Bunny All that grant you get—and you never seem to do anything.
Patrick It's not my fault.
Miss Blacklock Just enjoy your paper, Bunny . . .

Miss Blacklock gently pats Bunny's shoulder. Bunny opens the Gazette *and starts reading*

You *are* very lucky, Patrick . . .
Patrick I'm quite willing to go to more lectures.
Julia It's one giant holiday for him.
Patrick Oh, thanks for nothing—*sister*! Anyway listen to who's talking about a holiday—you've got the *whole* day off.
Julia Only because I've worked over-time—*every* night this week.
Patrick Huh! Pull the other one. I wouldn't be surprised if you haven't been working over-time at all. Been to the *pictures* more likely.

There is an odd glare between them. They hold it a moment

Miss Blacklock My goodness, you two—did you always bicker like this at home?
Julia *He* did. *I* didn't!

Quite suddenly Bunny sits upright

Bunny Letty! Letty!

Bunny's tone is enough to make Miss Blacklock get to her feet

Miss Blacklock What is it, Bunny? What's wrong?
Bunny Letty, dear. What does it mean?

Miss Blacklock moves to Bunny

Oh, my goodness. Whatever can it mean?
Miss Blacklock I won't know unless you tell me.

Bunny indicates the newspaper

Bunny Here. In the *Gazette*. Right at the bottom of the Personal Column.
Miss Blacklock Yes, dear?
Bunny It's an announcement . . .
Miss Blacklock How nice.

Bunny No, no—you don't understand . . .
Miss Blacklock No, I know I don't.
Bunny It says . . . Oh, dear—I can't bear to read it . .
Julia (*sweetly*) But, you will . . .

Bunny glares at Julia

Bunny Yes. (*Reading*) "A murder is announced and will take place on Friday, October the thirteenth, at Little Paddocks—at six-thirty p.m. Friends please accept this, the only intimation."

Bunny looks up at Miss Blacklock

Miss Blacklock Are you sure that's what it says?

Bunny indicates the newspaper

Bunny Right at the bottom . . .
Miss Blacklock This house? Little Paddocks?
Bunny Yes.
Patrick Read it again, Bunny.
Bunny (*reading*) "A murder is announced and will take place on Friday October the thirteenth . . .
Julia (*interrupting*) Today! I knew something dreadful was going to happen.
Miss Blacklock A few minutes ago you were complaining that *nothing* happened here. (*To Bunny*) Finish it.
Bunny (*reading*) ". . . at Little Paddocks at six-thirty p.m. Friends please accept this, the only intimation."

Bunny stops reading and looks around at them. It's an awkward moment as they look from one to the other

  Oh, Letty . . .
Miss Blacklock Let me see. (*She takes the newspaper from Bunny*)
Julia It's a joke.

Miss Blacklock looks up at her

  Well, it has to be. I mean, who'd be daft enough to advertise a *real* murder in the newspapers.
Patrick A madman might . . .
Miss Blacklock It's nothing to do with you, is it, Patrick?
Patrick I'm not potty.
Julia That's debatable.
Patrick Ho ho!
Miss Blacklock (*turning to Julia*) I wouldn't put it past you.

Julia is quickly on the defensive—perhaps a little too quickly

Julia It's nothing to do with me. Perhaps Phillipa can throw some light on it.
Patrick No, it's not the sort of thing she'd get up to, anyway.
Miss Blacklock I agree! Well *someone* seems to think it's amusing.
Bunny It frightens me.

Miss Blacklock It's nothing to worry about.
Bunny But what will happen at six-thirty?
Patrick Delicious Death!
Bunny (*hand to mouth*) Oh . . .
Miss Blacklock *Really*, Patrick!
Julia He means Mitzi's special cake. We always call it Delicious Death.
Patrick Yes Bunny. (*Reading*) "Friends, please accept this, the only
    intimation." Somebody's bound to drop round. I thought we might get
    her to make one.
Miss Blacklock I'm sure you did. (*To Bunny*) Nothing will happen at six-
    thirty, Bunny. Except Patrick is probably right in suggesting that one or
    two people might drop in out of curiosity.
Julia It might turn into a party.
Miss Blacklock It most certainly won't!
Patrick (*trying to make amends*) So, there's nothing to worry about,
    Bunny. Nothing.
Bunny *You really think so?*
Patrick Of course.
Bunny Oh, good. That makes me feel better.
Miss Blacklock We'll all laugh about it tomorrow, Bunny.
Bunny Yes. (*She starts to read again. The crisis is over*)

> *There is a moment's pause, then the Main Door opens and Mitzi, Miss
> Blacklock's cook enters, brandishing a copy of the* Gazette. *She is about
> twenty-five or twenty-six, small and dark—a mid-European, (Hungary,
> Roumania or perhaps Yugoslavia). She is an explosive character inclined
> to believe that everyone is against her. At the moment she is in one of her
> moods—upset and crackling*

Mitzi Someone is after me. I am going to be murdered in my bed!

Bunny is immediately alert to the tension

Bunny Murdered!
Mitzi It is here. In the *Gazette*. They are coming for me.
Miss Blacklock Whoever put that silly advert in the paper obviously did it
    with the precise intention of sending this house into total chaos!
Mitzi There will be blood everywhere. They will cut me up and feed me to
    the dogs.
Patrick Poor dogs!

Mitzi turns to him

Mitzi It will happen. In this very house. If I stay! *Tonight!* (*She waves the
    newspaper under his nose*) It is here—in this newspaper. They come to get
    me. At six-thirty tonight! You see—they care nothing for the law. They
    tell everyone they are coming to *murder* me . . . (*She goes into Hungarian*)
    Örulet örulet nire Kepesek . . .

Mitzi turns to leave, but Miss Blacklock stops her

Miss Blacklock No-one's going to murder you. It's a joke.

Mitzi I not laugh. I go!

Miss Blacklock Nevertheless, I don't think it has anything to do with you.

Mitzi You don't know. Once you have escaped—they never let you get away . . .

Bunny But I thought you did get away . . .

Mitzi They hound me. Day and night. Night and day. The telephone calls. You wonder what they are—who they are from . . .

Julia What telephone calls?

Mitzi Agents. From my country. Why? Why do you think they keep phoning me?

Bunny I expect they want to know how you're getting on over here, Millie.

Miss Blacklock But, Mitzi, I've never heard you get a telephone call.

Mitzi They do it in secret. They never leave me alone. They don't like it that I escape from them. Oh! You have no idea what it is like. They interrogate me. For days—weeks—months. The light shining in my eyes. My family—they send them to Siberia. (*She continues in Hungarian*) *De èn nem török meg! Nem mondom meg amit tudok. Tuljàrok az es-zukön es elszököm a szabad földre. Most jönnek utanam de en megyek!*

Miss Blacklock Mitzi! Do be sensible about this. Nothing is going to happen to you. No-one is going to come after you. No spy. No agent. So calm yourself down—we'll all look after you. Now. This is what I suggest you do. You get that beef out of the pantry and make that special goulash of yours for lunch.

There is a sudden and dramatic change in Mitzi's attitude

Mitzi Oh! You like my goulash—eh?

Miss Blacklock It's simply delicious.

Mitzi I make it even more special for you today. I put in some wine—some rich, red wine from Hungary . . . (*She kisses her fingers to express her feelings about the goulash*) It makes my mouth water just to think of it!

Miss Blacklock Good. You do that. Incidentally, I expect someone or other might be dropping in around six-thirty this evening.

But, even as she says this, Miss Blacklock regrets it. Mitzi immediately reacts

Mitzi To murder me!

Miss Blacklock (*irritatedly*) No, no, no!

Mitzi Why they come?

Miss Blacklock places a reassuring hand on Mitzi's shoulder

Miss Blacklock For a drink—and a sandwich perhaps. And you make such good sandwiches.

Mitzi (*still suspicious*) It will be all right?

Miss Blacklock There's nothing to worry about . . .

A moment, as Mitzi considers

Mitzi You are right. I am a good cook, no? I make a dip, too.

Miss Blacklock Well—yes. But not too much garlic, please.

Mitzi You not like garlic?

Miss Blacklock Well, yes—in moderation. But, after the last dip you made we were totally isolated in Church on Sunday—and that was two days after we'd eaten it!

Mitzi I tell you then. I use only two cloves of garlic this time—instead of my usual seven. But it not be nearly so good. I go now. Too long you have kept me gas-bagging.

With this Mitzi turns and exits quickly

Patrick claps his hands, applauding

Patrick Well done, Aunt Letty.

Julia Yes, beautifully handled.

Miss Blacklock How nice to have you two in agreement for once.

Bunny Letty was always very good with people. She could have gone a long way. Yes, a long way indeed—if only——

Miss Blacklock cuts across her quickly and we might spot just a slight meaningful glance

Miss Blacklock Now, now, Bunny dear. We mustn't keep reminiscing. Young people aren't interested in the past these days.

Bunny gets the message

Bunny (*flustered*) Dear me—I am so silly. I get so muddled lately. I am sorry, Letty. Really and truly sorry.

Miss Blacklock Bunny—I wasn't angry with you.

Bunny But, you're so right—everything's mixed up—I must be more careful—and think before I say something . . .

Miss Blacklock No one minds—we all understand. Read your paper, dear —you know how much you enjoy it.

Bunny Yes. That's what I'll do. But, I won't read that advertisement again, Letty.

Miss Blacklock (*a little despairingly*) No, dear—don't do that.

Bunny I shan't sleep a wink tonight though Mitzi could be right. We might all be murdered in our beds.

Miss Blacklock (*biting back the irritation*) No, dear, no. The advertisement says six-thirty. I don't think any of us will be in our beds by then.

Bunny (*after a moment*) Oh, no. We won't, will we?

Miss Blacklock So, there's nothing to worry about.

Bunny goes back to her paper. But, just as quickly, she puts it back down again

Bunny We could be murdered down here just as easily as upstairs!

Miss Blacklock Bunny!

Bunny Oh, no, don't do that Letty, please.

Miss Blacklock (*relenting*) Well, then.

Bunny goes back to the paper and stays reading it this time

Julia For a moment there I could see Mitzi clearing off and me having to do the cooking from now on . . . (*She turns sharply to Patrick*) And you needn't make any comment—thank you very much!
Patrick I was just thinking what a terrible liar Mitzi is.
Julia We all know she doesn't get any phone calls.
Patrick And what about her parents being sent to Siberia. Last time she told us they were executed in Red Square . . .
Julia While she stood there in the snow, with tears freezing on her cheeks.
Miss Blacklock We must be sympathetic towards her. She's lonely. Life must be pretty miserable with no-one you can talk to—no-one from your background. I suppose that's why she makes up all these stories.
Patrick Lies, you mean!
Miss Blacklock Yes, I do, But I think I can see why she does it.
Julia Why are her stories always such doom, gloom and disaster.
Miss Blacklock That's what she enjoys. Like some people enjoy reading murder mysteries.

There is a knock on the Main Door. It opens, and Miss Marple enters, carrying a bunch of violets wrapped in tissue paper. She is an elderly lady with an over-inquisitive mind which gets her into all sorts of trouble

Miss Marple The front door was open—I do hope I'm not intruding.
Miss Blacklock Not at all, Miss Marple . . .

Miss Marple moves into the room

Miss Marple Only I popped in to deliver these— (*she indicates the violets*) —to Miss Bunner . . .

Bunny beams brightly and gets to her feet

Bunny Oh—oh, how lovely . . .
Miss Marple You remember you admired them so at the Vicarage the other day. I told my nephew and he insisted I bring some along for you. (*She hands them to Bunny*)
Bunny How kind. How very kind. (*She holds them out to Miss Blacklock*) Look, Letty. Aren't they lovely? And so unusual in the autumn.
Miss Blacklock My grandmother was able to grow them right up to the winter months. I adore violets.
Miss Marple Yes, there's something very sentimental about them. Don't you think so, Julia?
Julia I think you have a very romantic nature, Miss Marple . . .
Miss Marple Do you?
Julia But, I do see what you mean.

Miss Marple is close enough to Patrick to give him a dig in the ribs

Miss Marple Well. I don't think Patrick does!
Julia There's no romance in *his* soul!
Miss Marple Well, you're only his sister—you probably wouldn't see it if it was there.

Bunny Where shall they go, Letty? I want everyone to enjoy them.

Miss Blacklock What about here on the sideboard? There's even a vase waiting for them.

Bunny And it's already got water in it. It must be stale. I'll get some fresh. Won't be a minute.

Bunny exits through Main Door with the violets and vase

Miss Blacklock Do sit down. I'm so glad you called. I wanted to ask you to Bunny's birthday party on Sunday. I know she'd love you to be here.

Miss Marple Thank you. I love parties. Perhaps there is something I can do to help.

Julia I'll be helping Aunt Letty, Miss Marple.

Patrick (*mimicking Julia*) I'll be helping Aunt Letty, Miss Marple.

Julia Well, you'll be in bed till noon and you'll spend the rest of the day snoring in an armchair—so we can't rely on you for any help!

Miss Marple The announcement in the *Gazette*. What does it mean?

Miss Blacklock You've seen that, have you?

Miss Marple I should think everybody in Chipping Cleghorn has seen it by now. Has it anything to do with Miss Bunner's birthday?

Julia We've no idea what it means.

Patrick Probably some crank who thinks he's being funny.

Miss Marple I see. I thought it was an invitation to play some sort of new game or something.

Patrick The murder game. Sounds good, doesn't it?

Miss Blacklock If you're interested Miss Marple, why don't you come along at six-thirty.

Julia Oh yes, do, Miss Marple.

Miss Marple I'd love to but I have to go into Medenham Wells for my treatment and I'm not sure how long it's going to take. I'll do my best, though.

Miss Blacklock Is your rheumatism better?

Miss Marple Very much, thank you. The spa waters are so good. Give it another week and I shall be back in St Mary Mead.

Patrick Chipping Cleghorn won't be the same without you!

Miss Marple I shall miss it here. Although I think my niece won't be over sorry when I leave. They've been very patient with me.

Julia Would they like to come tonight?

Miss Marple I'm sure they would love to. My nephew's very like me, he loves a mystery, but they're having dinner with the Bishop.

Julia It would have been rather reassuring to have the Vicar here.

Miss Marple Knowing your neighbours, you won't be alone. The Colonel and Mrs Easterbrook for a start . . .

Patrick No—they're in Bournemouth.

Miss Marple Clara Swettenham wouldn't miss an opportunity like this. And young Edmund—with two beautiful young girls staying here.

Julia There's someone I could do without. And Phillipa says he's a lay-about.

Miss Marple I thought he was a writer.

Julia He is. But, she says it's an excuse not to get a real job and work for a living.

Miss Marple (*smiling*) Perhaps she's got a point.

Bunny enters with the violets in the vase

Bunny Do thank the Vicar for me, Miss Marple. I'm touched—I really am. So kind of him.

Miss Marple He was delighted you noticed them. He brought the original cutting back from Devon—the Dart Valley—he was born there.

Bunny (*distantly*) Devon violets. There's nothing quite like them. (*She crosses to the bureau and "arranges" them on top—trying a couple of different places before she is satisfied*)

Miss Marple Well, I must be going. I hope all will be well this evening.

Bunny looks across—she has forgotten

Bunny (*smiling*) What?

Miss Marple The announcement—in the *Gazette*. A murder will take place here at six-thirty . . .

Bunny (*hand to mouth*) Oh—yes . . .

Miss Marple If it wasn't a joke or some sort of game it would be very worrying for all of you.

Miss Blacklock We're made of sterner stuff than you think, Miss Marple.

Miss Marple But, surely, Miss Blacklock. If there's going to be a murder there has to be a *victim*. If I were you the question I'd be asking myself is: who is going to be murdered?

A moment. They look from one to the other. We see the first signs of real fear beginning to creep into their souls, as—

the CURTAIN falls

SCENE 2

The same. It is six-ten that evening

Mitzi is putting things on the small centre table: glasses and drinks, sandwiches, the cheesy biscuits and the dip. Miss Blacklock is filling the silver cigarette-box on the table by the jutting out wall

Mitzi (*to Miss Blacklock*) You like what I do, Miss Blacklock. Yes?

Having finished filling the cigarette box, Miss Blacklock moves to Mitzi

Miss Blacklock Oh, yes—yes. Those do look nice, Mitzi. Thank you.

Mitzi The dip—well, it is not quite perfect. The sandwiches—in them I have put the pâté.

Miss Blacklock The pâté? Not my *pâté de fois gras*?

Mitzi It is delicious.

Miss Blacklock It was a present. It came from Fortnum's. I was saving that for a special occasion.

Mitzi You tell me to make sandwiches, I do it.

Miss Blacklock I was rather thinking of cheese.

Mitzi Huh! Your English cheese. It is like soap!

Miss Blacklock *We* like it.

Mitzi Do you need me anymore?

Miss Blacklock No, thank you, Mitzi. Are you going out?

Mitzi I have things to do in the dining-room. Then I go to my room and lock myself up.

Miss Blacklock (*smiling*) Before you go into hiding could you let the guests in when they arrive. I've decided to keep the front door locked this evening.

Mitzi (*explosively*) I am everything here. Head cook and bucket-washer.

Miss Blacklock Bottle-washer!

Mitzi Yes, that too!

With this Mitzi turns smartly and exits through the Main Door, as Julia enters

Julia Not long now . . . Aren't you worried?

Miss Blacklock (*after a moment*) Why should I be?

Julia Well, supposing this isn't a hoax. Supposing some maniac is going to commit a murder here tonight?

Miss Blacklock You're the last person I expected to take it seriously. (*She turns on the main light*)

Julia Well I do have a few butterflies in my stomach!

Miss Blacklock Well, have a drink and relax.

Julia What bothers me most is Miss Marple's comment.

Miss Blacklock Forget it. Miss Marple relishes this sort of thing. She's a real old busybody.

Julia But, quite a clever old busybody. And if she's right—who is going to be the victim?

Miss Blacklock (*impatiently*) No-one! Either it's a joke or it's someone who wants to get even. Someone I owe hospitality to and it's slipped my mind.

Julia But, if it isn't that—

Miss Blacklock (*irritatedly*) Julia . . .

Julia (*refusing to be stopped*)—One of us is going to die.

Miss Blacklock I *don't* want to hear any more—it's nonsense.

Julia It could be *you*! Or worse still *me!*

Miss Blacklock draws the window curtains

Miss Blacklock Oh, thank you very much.

Julia Well, it has to be someone in this house. Patrick—there are times when I could throttle him. Then there's Bunny.

Miss Blacklock Oh, perish the thought. Poor dear Bunny.

Julia I've seen you driven to distraction by her before now.

Miss Blacklock (*indignantly*) Yes, well . . . but we've been friends for years—from childhood. She can be irritating ... What a horrible thought.

Julia Well on a happier note perhaps it will be Mitzi who gets the chop. She gets on my nerves.

Miss Blacklock That's not a good enough reason to murder her.

Julia Phillipa puzzles me. Who is she? Where does she come from?

Miss Blacklock You know exactly who she is—and where she comes from.

Julia We've only got her word for it.

Miss Blacklock The same applies to you and Patrick ...

Julia But, Mother wrote to you—asked if we could stay here ...

Miss Blacklock How do I know it wasn't a forgery?

Julia I see what you mean. But it wasn't.

Miss Blacklock I'm sure it wasn't. The same way I'm sure about Phillipa.

Patrick enters by the Main Door, with Phillipa Haymes. She is a tall, rather elegant-looking blonde of about twenty-six, with a touch of real class about her—a young lady with a rather serious turn of mind

Patrick It's all going to take place at six-thirty and this room will be the scene of the crime, I suppose.

Phillipa This is a crazy story, Letty, it just doesn't make sense. If someone intends to commit a murder, why on earth announce it in a newspaper for everyone to see? I should have thought it would have been wise to keep quiet about it.

Julia You're right, Phillipa. It's crazy. It's got to be a mad man.

Patrick What about a mad woman?

Phillipa It's a wonder the police haven't been round here.

Miss Blacklock I shouldn't think for one moment they take it seriously.

Phillipa Do you?

A moment passes. Clearly, Miss Blacklock is worried

Miss Blacklock (*putting on a brave face*) Of course not. It's too silly for words.

Phillipa You don't sound too sure of yourself.

Miss Blacklock I certainly am! It's—it's just someone who wants an excuse for a drink. Let's forget it, shall we?

Patrick Poor Aunt Letty. It's rather getting on top of you, isn't it?

Miss Blacklock turns on him sharply

Miss Blacklock No, it isn't! But you keep going on about it. It's stupid and childish and I've heard enough. Do you understand?

Miss Blacklock has gone over the top. The three young people stare at her— aware that she is very rattled. Miss Blacklock realizes that she has gone too far and tries to cover up

   The Main Door opens and Bunny enters

Bunny Quack! Quack!

They all turn and stare at her

Quack! Quack! (*She stops and looks at them*) Quack!

Patrick gets the giggles and the girls stifle laughs

Miss Blacklock (*covering a smile*) Is anything wrong, Bunny?

Bunny Infernal noise they make, Letty. They're all out on the back lawn.

Miss Blacklock Oh, my goodness—the ducks. They should have been locked up ages ago. (*Suddenly, sharply*) Have you been outside like that?

Bunny What, Letty?

Miss Blacklock Without a coat.

Bunny (*guiltily*) Only to the bottom of the garden—to throw some rubbish away . . .

Miss Blacklock Dr Robinson would be very annoyed—and I'm not sure I shan't tell him!

Bunny Please don't . . .

Miss Blacklock You'll be the death of me! (*She suddenly realizes what she has said. Embarrassed*) I—I'd better lock them up. I'll only be a minute.

Phillipa I'll do it.

Miss Blacklock Certainly not, Phillipa. You've been at work all day. You relax.

Patrick I'll go.

Miss Blacklock Thank you, Patrick. But I'd rather do it myself.

Miss Blacklock exits through the Main Door

Bunny If I'd had my goloshes on I would have done it for her.

Patrick I noticed you stayed discreetly in the background. Afraid of getting your hands dirty?

Julia No. My new dress, as a matter of fact. (*She spins round to show off her skirt, which is a beautiful and clearly expensive kilt*)

Phillipa That must have cost a bomb.

Julia A *friend* bought it for me . . .

Phillipa Oh—like that, is it?

Julia Ask no questions . . .

Patrick (*imitating the Man in the Black Voice*) Death wore Black Chiffon.

Julia I beg your pardon.

Patrick If you're the murderer—Death wore Black Chiffon would be very appropriate, wouldn't it?

Julia If you're trying to be funny . . .

Bunny interrupts before Julia can finish

Bunny I once read a book called that.

Phillipa Are you sure, Bunny?

Bunny No. No, that wasn't it. Let me see. It was called—*Death Wore Black Lingerie*.

They all look at her in amazement. She looks up at them smiling benignly

(*After a moment of thought*) No, no. I'm wrong. *Death Wore a Bra and Panties*. That's it. Definitely. Nice book—though there were some parts that I didn't quite understand. (*She beams at them*)

The Main Doors open and Miss Blacklock enters

Miss Blacklock There is something you can do for me, Patrick.
Patrick Anything.
Miss Blacklock (*going to the drinks*) There's not much sherry. (*She picks up a bottle*) Put this away and get a new one please.

Patrick looks at the bottle, puzzled

Patrick There's more than half a bottle.
Miss Blacklock It's been open a long time . . .

She hands the bottle to him. He takes the bottle and looks at it, even more puzzled

Patrick But . . . (*He checks himself and goes to the door*)

As Patrick reaches the Main Door it opens and Mitzi enters. She stands there like an usher about to make an announcement

Mitzi (*trying to be dignified*) Here are Mrs Swettenham and her son Edmund Swettenham. Thank you. You're welcome.

Julia has to turn her back. Phillipa just manages to keep a straight face.

Patrick laughs. Mitzi is furious

Why you laugh at me?
Patrick (*controlling himself*) It wasn't you—it was something else—honest.
Mitzi You—you keep out of my kitchen!
Miss Blacklock Mitzi!

Mitzi turns, and almost knocks the Swettenhams flying as she exits

Mitzi This way, please.

Mitzi exits. Mrs Swettenham and Edmund enter. She is a woman in her late fifties. He is twenty-six or twenty-seven, a serious young man with pretensions of being a writer. He has not had anything published yet. He is dark and somewhat foreign-looking, although he is, in fact, very English

Miss Blacklock moves up to greet them

Miss Blacklock Clara. Edmund. How nice of you to call.
Mrs Swettenham (*awkwardly*) We were—just passing—Letty . . .
Miss Blacklock *Really?*
Mrs Swettenham That's right—isn't it, Edmund?

She turns to Edmund for support, but clearly his heart is not in it

Edmund Yes, Mother—that's right.

Patrick exits through the Main Door

Mrs Swettenham We were in the car and I said to Edmund—who drives much too fast, you know—"Oh, look, Edmund. We're passing Little

Paddocks. Letty would never forgive us if we didn't drop in and say
hello." And Edmund said . . . (*She turns to him again*) What was it you
said?

He swallows hard. Clearly, he is embarrassed

Edmund "What a good idea."
Mrs Swettenham And I said—"Yes, isn't it". So, here we are.
Miss Blacklock Well, it was very nice of you to think of us. Do sit down.
  (*To Bunny*) Isn't it, Bunny?
Bunny What is, Letty?
Miss Blacklock Clara and Edmund were just passing and decided to drop
  in and see how we were.
Bunny Oh, but this morning you said they'd be bound to call in—bursting
  with curiosity you said—after seeing the announcement in the *Gazette*.
  You did see it, didn't you, Clara?

If the ground could open up and swallow all of them, it would be merciful

Mrs Swettenham Well, I er—that is—was it the one . . .
Bunny Right at the bottom of the Personal Column . . .

  Patrick enters with a bottle of sherry

Mrs Swettenham Oh, yes. I may have noticed it . . . (*She gives a nervous
  little laugh*)
Bunny Julia said you'd be here, too. Wild horses, wouldn't keep you
  away . . .

*Mrs Swettenham and Julia smile sweetly at each other. Miss Blacklock
attempts to ease the embarrassment*

Miss Blacklock Well, anyway—now that you are here . . .
Patrick (*picking up*) Totally unexpected.
Miss Blacklock (*glaring at him*) Patrick! Er—let's all have a drink.
Patrick Um?
Miss Blacklock *Drinks.*
Patrick (*waking up*) Yes, of course. Sherry, Mrs Swettenham?

*Miss Blacklock leads Mrs Swettenham and Edmund across to the bay
window*

Mrs Swettenham (*still a little put out*) Well, um—yes, that will be fine,
  thank you.
Patrick Edmund?
Edmund Thank you.

*Patrick busies himself at the sideboard getting drinks for everyone. Edmund,
still embarrassed, turns his attention to Phillipa*

  Well, Phillipa. You looked very busy this morning.
Phillipa Things got even more hectic after you left.
Julia (*seizing on it*) I see. You two have been having *secret* meetings, eh?
  Hatching something?

Phillipa (*seething*) There was nothing *secret* about it and we're not hatching anything.

Edmund (*still embarrassed*) No, no. By no means. You see, I had to call at Dayas Hall with some honey for Mrs Lucas.

Julia That's *your* story.

Phillipa Julia . . .

Julia Yes, darling?

Phillipa I should be careful. Otherwise a few things might come out that the rest of us would consider most peculiar . . .

Patrick steps in fast with the drinks to stop a storm blowing up

Patrick Drinks, everyone!

Patrick hands Mrs Swettenham and Edmund their drinks; then Miss Blacklock and Bunny. He hands a glass each to Julia and Phillipa

Cheers!

They take their drinks, still angry with one another and are about to drink

I've laced yours with a dash of cyanide!

This stops them in mid-action, but Patrick raises his glass to them and to the others. The others return his greeting but the two girls are still a bit dubious. Then Julia decides to take the plunge

Julia Oh, well—you can only die once. Cheers!

Julie drinks and Phillipa follows her example. Julie indicates to them to move back to the main part of the drawing-room. While they are taking up various positions in the room, Miss Blacklock crosses to the cigarette-box on the small table. Patrick remains near the drinks. Bunny goes to her chair, which is positioned so that she is in the best possible place to see Miss Blacklock. Phillipa and Edmund move so that they are in a direct line with the Main Door. Miss Blacklock crosses to Phillipa with the cigarette-box. Phillipa takes one and Edmund lights it for her with a match

Bunny Letty?

Miss Blacklock Yes?

Bunny When is this murder going to take place?

Mrs Swettenham Six-thirty . . . (*She realizes she has jumped in too quickly for someone who was "just passing" and not too concerned*)

Bunny (*to Mrs Swettenham*) Are you the murderer?

Mrs Swettenham is startled by Bunny's directness—so is everyone else

Mrs Swettenham Me? Of course I'm not?

Bunny Well, you seem to know all about it.

Mrs Swettenham (*flustered*) Well, er—it was in the *Gazette*—wasn't it?

Miss Blacklock (*helping out*) I wouldn't be surprised if everyone in Chipping Cleghorn saw it this morning.

Mrs Swettenham (*thankfully*) Yes—yes, indeed . . .

Miss Blacklock indicates the clock

Miss Blacklock It's nearly six-thirty, and if it's going to happen at all it'll
be any moment now. Cigarette, anyone?

Mrs Swettenham No, thank you.

Phillipa Yes please, Letty.

*Miss Blacklock crosses to Phillipa and offers a cigarette to Phillipa who
takes one. Edmund lights it for her*

Thank you, Edmund.

*The clock starts to chime the half-hour. All eyes turn to look at it. Every-
body freezes: transfixed by the clock. We can almost feel the tension. As the
last chime rings out, the lights go out leaving the room in total darkness*

*We hear Bunny gasp (almost a scream). One or two voices speak out:
"What's happening?", "Who's put the lights out?" "Come on—you've had
your joke. Put them back on", "For goodness sake, stop playing around. It's
not funny anymore", and so on*

  *Then the Main Door bursts open with a crash, and a powerful flashlight
  plays round the room. The man holding the flashlight is Rudi Scherz—a
  young Swiss national*

Scherz (*barking*) Get your hands up! Stay where you are!

*The flashlight lands on Julia. Her hands are still by her side—she is very
cool*

  (*more angrily*) I said: Get your hands up! If you want to get out of this
  alive do as you're told.

*His tone of voice is such that Julia obeys instantly. The flashlight moves on to
Mrs Swettenham who gives a startled gasp, but whose hands would touch the
ceiling if she could make them do so. The light now swings on to Edmund—
but he has made only a half-hearted attempt to obey the order*

You! High! High above your head!

*The menace in this man's voice leaves no doubt in Edmund's mind. His hands
shoot up. Bunny is shaking with fear and is out of her chair and standing on
tip-toe in an effort to do as she is told. The light swings from her and lands on
Patrick who, for once, is behaving himself*

You, away from the door. Go.

*The light stays on Patrick briefly and then moves on to just about where Miss
Blacklock is standing*

Now!

*At this point, we hear firstly two shots fired—then a tiny pause—followed by
a third shot. There are several screams, then, the flashlight falls to the
ground and spins round before going out, and at the same time we hear a
heavy thud. Then there is silence, held for a moment until Julia breaks it*

Julia For God's sake. Someone put the lights on!

Mrs Swettenham Has he gone?

Phillipa I can't see—have you got those matches Edmund?

Edmund searches for a moment

Edmund Blast! That was the last one.
Mrs Swettenham Someone put the lights on . . .
Patrick They must be fused.
Edmund Where's the fuse-box?
Patrick In the hall—I'll go.

We hear Patrick cross the room and stumble

What the hell?
Julia What is it?
Patrick Stay calm. I'll soon have the lights back on.

Patrick exits through the Main Door

Bunny (*tremulously*) Letty . . . (*She waits for a moment or two—there is no reply*) Letty . . . ?
Miss Blacklock It's all right, Bunny—stay calm.
Bunny I'm frightened . . .
Miss Blacklock (*strained*) There's no need . . .

A moment, and then the Lights come on

Edmund He's unconscious. Must have knocked himself out.

Patrick enters

Patrick Who is it?
Edmund I've no idea. Better get his gun—before he comes round.
Patrick Yes . . . (*He spots the gun by Rudi Scherz, and is about to pick it up but checks himself. He takes a handkerchief from his pocket and picks the gun up by the barrel*)
Miss Blacklock Will someone please help me.

All eyes turn to Miss Blacklock and ignore the body of Rudi Scherz on the floor. Miss Blacklock has blood all down the side of her face and all over her white blouse. It is a very dramatic sight so it is easy for them all to ignore Scherz for the moment

Bunny (*horrified*) Letty . . .

Everyone moves to her as she sways unsteadily on her feet. They crowd round her, firing questions: "Is she badly hurt?" "It looks terrible", "Someone get her a brandy", and so on

Phillipa Brandy? We'd better call a doctor.
Miss Blacklock No! I shall be all right . . .

At the same time we hear banging on a door off and Mitzi screaming—but quite distant. No-one takes any notice at this stage. Julia and Phillipa help Miss Blacklock to a chair

Miss Blacklock It's nothing—just my ear . . .

Edmund notices Patrick holding the gun in the handkerchief

Edmund Why the handkerchief?

Patrick (*indignantly*) I don't suppose the police would be very happy if I got my fingerprints all over it.

Mrs Swettenham Police?

Edmund They'll have to be called in, mother.

The banging on the door and the shouting off continues. Phillipa turns to it

Phillipa Is that Mitzi?

Patrick Yes. Someone seems to have locked her in the dining-room.

Phillipa Why do that?

Patrick I've no idea.

Phillipa Hadn't we better let her out?

Julia I'll do it.

Patrick No. There might be a . . . I'll do it in a moment.

Mrs Swettenham Are you feeling better, Letty?

Miss Blacklock (*with a thin smile*) Thank you . . .

> *Miss Marple enters, with Mitzi close behind*

Miss Marple What happened?

Julia Aunt Letty's been shot at.

Miss Marple bends down to examine Rudi Scherz, who is at her feet

Miss Marple By this man?

Patrick moves to her and the body. Mitzi is frozen to the spot

Patrick Of course! Is he coming round?

Miss Marple (*looking up*) No.

Patrick I wonder who he is?

Miss Marple I know who he is.

They all turn to look at Miss Marple

His name is Rudi Scherz—(*pause*)—and he's dead!

CURTAIN

SCENE 3

The same. The following Saturday morning

As the CURTAIN *goes up, Inspector Craddock is lying in the same position as the body in the previous scene. Sergeant Mellors is standing below the sideboard looking at Craddock. Craddock, a man of about fifty, rises and looks at the bullet holes in the wall by the sideboard*

Craddock So. He fires two shots from here—hits the wall—and then shoots himself?

Mellors If he tripped, he could have done it accidentally, sir.

Craddock Are they all here, now?

Mellors Yes, sir. Grumbling and moaning . . .

Craddock (*with apparent uninterest*) Oh . . .

Mellors And I should watch that Edmund Swettenham.

Craddock Why?

Mellors I should think he's a bit of a left-wing intellectual.

Craddock I didn't get that impression last night.

Mellors He's been a bit bolshy with me, sir. He was having a go at the Force this morning. Sprouting on about our Gestapo methods.

Craddock Oh—Christ! Why do I always pick the awkward ones?

Mellors You do seem to attract them, sir.

Craddock Why can't I get a nice, peaceful, law-abiding lot who do as they're told and answer my questions with a certain amount of civility.

Mellors Not your style, sir.

Craddock Once! Just once! That's all I ask. (*He looks up, pointing*) Somebody up there doesn't like me, Sergeant. And, what's more— (*indicating off*)—that lot out there are trying to compound the felony.

Mellors (*after a moment*) Shall I wheel them in?

Craddock There's nothing else for it, is there?

Mellors 'Fraid not, sir.

Mellors goes to the Locked Door and tries to open it

Craddock Not that door, it's been sealed for years.

Mellors goes out through the Main Door and across to the dining-room, asking the people to come through into the drawing-room. They do so, everyone who was in the room at the close of the previous scene, chattering amongst themselves as they enter

(*In a normal voice*) Can I have your attention, please?

They take no notice

Quiet, please.

They still take no notice

(*Shouting*) Perlease!

They are all a little taken aback. The chatter dies instantly

That's very good of you. I do appreciate your co-operation.

Mrs Swettenham This is very inconvenient, Inspector. It is Saturday. There's shopping, and lots of jobs to be done.

Craddock I understand your problem, Mrs Swettenham. But, may I remind you, a man died here last night—right on the spot where you're standing—

A little horrified at the thought, Mrs Swettenham shifts her position

—and whilst it may not seem overly important to you—it is to me and society in general. So, if it's not asking too much I'd like you to push your shopping to the back of your mind for a while and answer a few questions.

Edmund (*irritatedly*) I would have thought there were enough questions asked last night . . .

Craddock Ah, well—perhaps you don't think the same way as me, young man. Yes, I should think that's the answer—we think differently. But, if you cast your mind back—way, way back to last night—you'll surely recall that I allowed you all to go home and get some rest on the understanding that you'd co-operate fully this morning.

Edmund Well, it's perfectly clear what happened. This man—Scherz was his name, I believe—

Craddock Yes.

Edmund —broke in here—intending to steal—from Miss Blacklock—or the rest of us—fired the shots to scare us—tripped in the dark—and killed himself, poor devil.

Craddock eyes him for a moment

Craddock I understand you're a bit of a writer?

Edmund (*embarrassedly*) Well, er—yes—I do write . . .

Craddock Well, I hope all your plots aren't as obvious as that—otherwise I don't think I'll be very interested in reading any of your books!

Julia stifles a laugh

Now, er—perhaps we could get on with this—

Miss Blacklock I'm sure we're all perfectly willing to do anything you ask, Inspector. But, it has been quite a shock to us, you know . . .

Craddock I appreciate that, Miss Blacklock. But, you see, for a start—he didn't break in. No locks broken. No windows forced . . .

Miss Marple He must have come in by the back door—I did.

Craddock (*to Miss Blacklock*) And, as I was saying when Miss Marple interrupted me, there's your very bad habit of leaving the doors unlocked for *all and sundry* to come and go as they please.

Miss Blacklock I locked the front door—

Craddock For once . . .

Miss Blacklock —and everyone in the village does it—leaves them open, I mean.

Craddock Foolish—very foolish.

Miss Blacklock I suppose I must have left the back door open when I went to lock up the ducks . . .

Craddock Now, Miss Blacklock, last night you said you knew this Rudi Scherz.

Miss Blacklock Hardly knew, Inspector. His father owned a small hotel in Montreux. I spent many years in Switzerland helping to nurse my sister and I used to have a meal there occasionally. Recently, I had lunch in The Royal Spa Hotel in Medenham Wells. He was there. He approached me—said he recognized me and that he was over here to get a thorough grounding in the hotel business. However, I must point out that I had no recollection of him at all. But a few days later he called on me here . . .

Craddock He's been here before?

Miss Blacklock Yes.

Bunny I remember, Letty. You were very upset. He asked you for some money.

Miss Blacklock That's right. He gave me some story about his father being taken seriously ill and he desperately needed money for his air fare. Well I believed he was lying. After all, if his father owned a hotel, surely his family could afford to send him the fare? I told him I had no intention of lending him money. What surprised me most was that he didn't make a fuss. He just left—like a lamb.

Craddock I see. Do you think he may have called here purely to look around? See what the layout of the house was? That sort of thing.

Miss Blacklock Well. I haven't given it much thought—until now. I suppose that's what he must have been up to. Not that it would have done him any good. I don't keep more than a few pounds in the house.

Craddock Valuables?

Miss Blacklock Nothing.

Craddock Jewellery? Silver?

Miss Blacklock Nothing worth a great deal. Little bits and pieces. The silver's reasonable—nothing more. Mitzi was cleaning it last night . . .

Mitzi instantly springs to life

Mitzi I not touch it! It is nothing to you Secret Police officers. You come here. You blame me all the time. It was the same where I come from. Torture. Interrogation. But, I do not crack. You understand. I do not break. I tell them nothing. (*She stamps her foot and stands there defiantly with her hands on her hips*) Yah!

Craddock stands there for a moment, long-suffering, then appeals to the others

Craddock Is she always like this?

Mitzi Torture me! You get nowhere! I am innocent! Innocent! I was locked in the dining-room. That—is my hundred-per-cent alibi—as you say!

Craddock And a very good alibi it is. Perhaps too good on the surface. Now just sit down. And try to remember that I'm not too keen on the histrionics . . .

Mitzi (*still furious*) I will not . . .

Craddock Ah—ah—ah! (*Firmly*) Sit!

Mitzi sits, like a lamb

Craddock Let me say this to all of you. I don't want to be here anymore than you do. There's a very good football match on at Milchester this afternoon I'd very much like to see. But, other things are more—pressing. *Please.* Can we continue this interrogation without any more interruptions? Miss Blacklock. We've established that you knew Rudi Scherz.

Miss Marple Excuse me, Inspector. I'm sorry to interrupt. I knew him, too.

Craddock looks along the length of his nose at her. Another interruption! Miss Marple smiles sweetly at him

Craddock You didn't mention this last night.

Miss Marple I did—but, you weren't here at the time. And, well—when you arrived you rather neglected me.

Craddock Did I Oh . . .!

Miss Marple Probably because I didn't arrive until after the, er—action— took place.

Craddock Hm—rather like turning to the end of the book to see who the killer is, eh?

This is the start of their relationship. A rapport which builds as the story unfolds

Miss Marple As analogy it doesn't work. Because that's cheating. I usually guess who it is without resorting to those tactics. Do you turn to the last page?

Craddock (*sniffing*) If only I could. You, er—knew Rudi Scherz, you said?

Miss Marple I stayed at the Royal Spa whilst I was having intensive treat- ment—for rheumatism. He made up my bill.

Craddock (*knowingly*) Ah.

Miss Marple There were one or two—discrepancies—which I couldn't fail to notice, of course.

Craddock Of course.

Miss Marple It was clear to me that he was "on the make", as they say in the trade. Naturally, when the errors were pointed out he apologized profusely. But, we both knew.

Craddock Did you report him?

Miss Marple There was nothing I could actually *prove*.

Craddock He does seem to have been a bit of a villain. I'll know more soon. The Swiss police are running a check on him. (*Pause*) I'd like you all to take up the exact positions you were in last night as far as possible, that is—when the shots were fired.

Miss Marple Do you want me to leave? I was coming up the drive.

Craddock So you were outside when you heard the shots were you?

Miss Marple I was, Inspector. As you will realize I came in through the back door. Mitzi was banging about in the dining-room. I let her out and then we both came in here.

Craddock Tell you what you can do. Keep an eye on her. I don't want her banging about again.

Mitzi (*bristling*) I am not banging about—(*she carries on in Hungarian*)— *mindig en vagyok a hiba's* . . .

Craddock Shush—shush—shush . . .!

Mitzi Ah . . .

Craddock And shush again!

Miss Marple takes Mitzi by the arm and leads her to the sofa by the window

Miss Marple Come and sit down, Mitzi . . .
Craddock Now come along everyone, perlease.

The others now start to take up their positions

Thank you. Thank you very much. (*He goes to the Main Door*) The lights go out—and a flashlight comes on, then lands on—you! (*He points to Julia*)
Julia My hands weren't up. I thought it was a joke. Then he—barked at me. I was so frightened I put my hands up so high—like this . . . (*She demonstrates*)
Craddock He couldn't complain at that, could he?

Julia drops her hands

Julia I thought he was going to shoot me.
Craddock You're Miss Blacklock's niece. Right?
Julia (*puzzled and hesitant*) Well—yes . . .
Craddock That's the sort of answer I like. Full of confidence. You *are* Miss Blacklock's niece?
Julia (*indignantly*) It's just that I don't see what my relationship with Aunt Letty has to do with it.
Craddock May I suggest that you leave me to work that out? In any case. I was merely trying to establish who you are.
Julia You can check up on it if you like.
Craddock I will. Your mother lives in the south of France I understand?
Julia (*nervously*) She's lived there for some time. It suits her health.
Craddock (*after a moment*) Thank you. Mrs Swettenham?
Mrs Swettenham Yes?

They regard each other for a brief moment

Craddock The light moved on to you next, Mrs Swettenham?
Mrs Swettenham I was totally dazzled. I couldn't see anything. I just heard that voice—frightening—gutteral . . .
Craddock You haven't all that long returned to this country. Is that right?
Mrs Swettenham Yes. My husband was in the Diplomatic Service. He died abroad. Naturally, I returned with Edmund . . .
Craddock Where were you—abroad, that is?
Mrs Swettenham (*bothered*) Why? Turin. My husband was with the Trade Delegation there. (*Clearly worried by this line of interrogation*) I don't see what my personal life has got to do with this.

Craddock ignores her last remark

Craddock If my knowledge of geography hasn't entirely deserted me— Turin is not all that far from the Swiss border, is it?
Mrs Swettenham No.
Craddock Thank you, Mrs Swettenham.

Edmund springs to her defence

Edmund Just what are you insinuating?

Craddock turns slowly to face him, and looks at him for a moment

Craddock The light fell on you next, didn't it?
Edmund (*very definitely*) Yes, it did!
Craddock Thank you very much.

With this he turns and ignores him

Edmund Aren't you going to ask me any more questions?
Craddock Not right now. (*He turns back to face Phillipa*) Mrs Haymes. The light never fell on you at all, did it?
Phillipa No, it didn't.
Craddock You were actually facing the door.
Phillipa That's right . . .
Craddock Was it possible to see this man at all?
Phillipa Not really—it was difficult to see anything.
Craddock But, you were in a good position.
Phillipa It was very dark—I suppose I could make out a shape—but nothing more.
Craddock (*after a moment*) How long ago did your husband die?

This question seems to throw Phillipa

Phillipa (*startled*) Why? What on earth has it got to do with this?
Craddock I'd like to know when and why you came to live here.
Phillipa I still don't see what the relevance is . . .

Craddock moves so that he is closer to her. Clearly, it makes her feel uneasy

Craddock Does it strike you as odd that virtually all of you are *newcomers* to Chipping Cleghorn?

A moment. They all feel a little uncomfortable

Phillipa It's—never occurred to me until now.
Craddock Odd though . . .
Phillipa I came here a few months ago because I was offered a job. Restoring the gardens at Dayas Hall. I'm a trained horticulturist.
Craddock That's nice. Gardener! (*He turns his attention to Bunny*) Miss Bunner.
Bunny You've not going to give me the third degree are you, Inspector?
Craddock (*smiling*) Not today. But, if you can tell me what you saw—if anything—I'd be very grateful. You were in a good position to see Miss Blacklock and the gunman if the lights had been on.
Bunny (*pleased*) Yes, I was.
Craddock I want you to think very hard and tell me what you saw *before* the lights went out.
Bunny Before?
Craddock Yes. Then we'll see what you remember after the lights went out.
Bunny Let me see—Letty was holding the vase . . .
Miss Blacklock No, Bunny, dear. I was holding the cigarette-box. I'd been handing them round.

Bunny looks puzzled

Bunny (*thoughtfully*) I remember now. You were holding the cigarette-box, not the vase.

Craddock Then what, Miss Bunner?

Bunny The flash . . .

Craddock From the torch?

Bunny No . . .

Craddock Oh?

Bunny There was a flash. It must have been the light on the cigarette-box. We always keep it polished.

Craddock Ah . . .

Bunny Then it was dark—and he fired his gun at poor Letty. How could anyone do that?

Craddock You actually saw him fire the gun?

Bunny I saw the gun fire at Letty.

Craddock Thank you, Miss Bunner.

Bunny He should be locked up.

Julia Bunny, he's dead.

Bunny Serves him right. He tried to murder Letty.

Craddock moves to Patrick

Craddock *You* were by the door. Having a few drinks?

Patrick I only had one, you know.

Craddock Whatever you say. But, you were by the door.

Patrick No. I was by the door but he told me to move away from it. After the first two shots, he brushed past me and I tried to trip him up.

Craddock That's when you think he fell?

Patrick Yes, I suppose so.

Craddock And after that you went out to mend the fuse?

Patrick Yes. I didn't mend it. I simply switched the fuses around. It was quicker and easier. It was easy for me, of course. I knew exactly where the fuse-box was—how to open it—and which circuit was affected . . . (*He trails off*)

A moment's pause. Patrick licks his lips nervously

Craddock You're Miss Simmons' brother?

Patrick (*still nervously*) Um—I'm a year older . . .

Craddock Miss Blacklock's nephew?

Patrick Er, no . . .

Craddock I understood you were.

Miss Blacklock We're second cousins, Inspector. Patrick's mother is my first cousin . . .

Patrick We call her Aunt because our mother always referred to her as that . . . So, when we came to live here—(*he shrugs his shoulders*)—well . . .

Craddock How long have you been living here?

Patrick Three months—I should think.

Craddock So the three of you have only really known each other since about June or July this year?

Miss Blacklock I did know them as children . . .

Craddock Mmm. I see. (*To Miss Blacklock*) Would you mind standing in the exact position you were in when the shots were fired, please?

Miss Blacklock looks at the wall, shuffles her feet and checks again to see that she is in position. Craddock moves to her and traces the path the bullet would have taken before it entered the wall. He does it for each hole. We see that one could very easily have nicked her ear

Well. That was a very narrow escape, wasn't it?

Miss Blacklock I was extremely fortunate.

Craddock turns from her to address the others

Craddock Right. Well, that wasn't too painful, was it?

Julia We can go?

Craddock You can. But, do all stay in the village, won't you? Don't take a sudden and unexpected holiday or anything like that.

Miss Marple Excuse me, Inspector?

Craddock Yes, Miss Marple?

Miss Marple You haven't questioned me.

Craddock But, you didn't turn up until after the, er—action!

Miss Marple (*a tinge indignantly*) Suppose I was lying? Suppose I was Rudi Scherz' accomplice? I could easily have locked Mitzi in the dining-room. I could have hidden for a while—I know the layout of the house—then pretended to turn up after it was all over?

Craddock In that case, I'll put you under arrest!

Miss Marple (*astonished*) But, I didn't—and I wasn't his accomplice!

Craddock In that case, you're free to go!

Miss Marple is irritated that he has been getting at her—teasing her

Miss Marple How very disappointing. You're having a game with me, Inspector.

Craddock And you with me, Miss Marple. I shall question you—when I'm ready.

Miss Marple Very well.

Craddock Thank you everyone—I shall be talking to you all again soon. Miss Blacklock, I'd like you to stay.

Everyone files out except Craddock and Miss Marple

Sit down, please, Miss Blacklock.

Miss Blacklock goes to a chair, clearly a little nervous. He moves to sit opposite her. A moment, as they sit facing each other. A little tension starting to creep in

(*Seriously*) Miss Blacklock . . .

Miss Blacklock (*nervously*) Yes . . .

Craddock I think it's cards on the table time.

Miss Blacklock (*warily*) I don't understand, Inspector.
Craddock I think you do.

Another moment passes—more tension builds up

Someone tried to kill you last night.
Miss Blacklock (*exclaiming*) Oh no! No, Inspector!
Craddock I think there's no doubt of it.
Miss Blacklock But, *why*?
Craddock I hope we're going to find out.
Miss Blacklock I think you're wrong, Inspector. There were plenty of opportunities for Rudi Scherz to kill me if he wanted to. Why wait till last night? Why invite witnesses?
Craddock What makes you think it was Rudi Scherz?
Miss Blacklock Well—wasn't it?
Craddock He did place the advertisement in the *Gazette*.
Miss Blacklock Well, there you are. It sort of—proves my point. If he'd wanted to kill me, why not wait behind a hedge and pop me off when no-one was about? No, I'm sorry, Inspector. I think you're wrong. He didn't come here to kill me.

Pause

Craddock Someone could have put him up to it.
Miss Blacklock (*puzzled*) Put him up to it?
Craddock Someone who wanted you dead—and is prepared to pay Rudi Scherz to do the job. You see, I'm not so sure *his* death was an accident.
Miss Blacklock How could it be anything else? He tripped and shot himself.
Craddock No. Supposing there was someone else. And what if this someone assumed that he'd done his job and killed you? Wouldn't it be safer to shoot Rudi Scherz so that there was no possibility of him getting caught by the police and telling us the truth?
Miss Blacklock I see exactly what you are saying, Inspector.
Craddock You agree with me then?
Miss Blacklock No. Because *why*? Why should anyone want to kill me.
Craddock I've a feeling you might be able to answer that.
Miss Blacklock I can't. I've no enemies that I know of. I'm on friendly terms with everyone in the village. It's too ridiculous.

There is a pause. Craddock considers his next move

Craddock Who gets your money if you die?

Miss Blacklock takes a deep breath

Miss Blacklock Is this *really* necessary, Inspector?
Craddock Perlease, Miss Blacklock. Indulge me. Answer my question.

She considers for a moment

Miss Blacklock (*reluctantly*) Patrick and Julia . . .
Craddock I see.

Miss Blacklock (*angrily*) I might add that the furniture and a small annuity goes to—Miss Bunner. So I suppose she becomes a suspect, too! The point is—there really isn't much to leave. Frankly, I'm not *worth* murdering.

Craddock But, nevertheless, all *three* of them benefit.

Miss Blacklock And not *one* of them would harm a hair on my head!

Craddock You'd be surprised what people will do for money.

Miss Blacklock loses her cool. She gets up and moves away from him in an attempt to bring the interview to an end

Miss Blacklock Really, Inspector—I find this conversation extremely distasteful. You are accusing people very dear to me. People I trust—yes, with my life!

There is a pause. Each is wary of the other

Craddock Have you got anything of great value?

Miss Blacklock (*irritatedly*) Nothing special—nothing out of the ordinary...

Craddock (*indicating*) Those pearls you're wearing?

Miss Blacklock's hand goes up to her throat in a reflex action—just to touch them for a second

Miss Blacklock They *are priceless* ...

Craddock (*on his toes*) Oh?

Miss Blacklock But only to me. They belong to my sister. We were very close. I wear them all the time. They somehow—and I don't suppose you'll understand this for one minute—keep me in touch with her ...

Craddock (*after a moment*) I like to think I'm not insensitive. But, I still think someone is trying to kill you. Can you come back to the wall, please.

They go to the wall where the bullets entered

If he'd merely intended to frighten you and everyone else, he could have fired the shots into the ceiling. But, think. The clock struck the half-hour. Everybody turned to it. The lights went out. The door swung open ...

As he says this, the Main Door starts to swing open. Miss Blacklock gasps. Craddock's jaw drops open

> *Finally, the Main Door swings fully open to reveal—Miss Marple, who is standing there with a toy gun in one hand and a torch in the other*

Miss Blacklock Miss Marple!

Miss Marple moves into the room, looking quite menacing

Craddock Give me that gun!

Miss Marple It's a toy. It fires pieces of potato.

Craddock What is this all about?

Miss Marple I couldn't help wondering how that young man could be in three places at once—fusing the lights, locking Mitzi in the dining-room and opening the door with a gun in one hand and a torch in the other. I couldn't. I had to put the gun down, open the door and pick it up after. It seems to me he was a very athletic young man.

Craddock Good point, Miss Marple.

Miss Marple Inspector—that's praise indeed. Tell me, do you think it's possible that Rudi Scherz had an accomplice?

Craddock Miss Marple?

Miss Marple Yes?

Craddock Would you like my job?

Miss Marple Yes, but I'd never make a policeman.

Craddock You think not?

Miss Marple I'm not tall enough. I started on that little charade in the hope that it might help to prove my theory that Rudi Scherz came here to murder Miss Blacklock . . .

Craddock I've been trying to convince her of that myself. Perhaps now you'll believe that it's not the ranting of an hysterical old copper. Someone is waiting to murder you and it can happen anytime now!

Miss Blacklock Just because Miss Marple agrees with you—it doesn't mean to say you're right.

Craddock I'm trying to save your life.

Miss Marple I believe that, too, Miss Blacklock.

Craddock *Somewhere* there's a reason. And *you* know it—it may be hidden deep in your mind—we've got to bring it out.

Miss Blacklock (*hesitantly*) There's no reason—I'm sure . . .

Craddock Perlease! Think!

Miss Marple But—I understand that one day you could inherit millions.

There is a stunned silence

Craddock Miss Marple?

Miss Blacklock stares at Miss Marple who feels more than a little uncomfortable

Miss Marple Miss Bunner was telling me when we were having coffee in the Blue Bird Coffee House . . .

Miss Blacklock Trust Bunny! I shall have to do something about her!

Craddock Why have you been keeping something back from me?

Miss Blacklock It's *nothing*. It doesn't concern this case or you! In fact, it's most unlikely to happen.

Craddock Do I have to ask Miss Marple or Miss Bunner for the details?

There is a pause. Craddock is seething

Miss Blacklock (*coolly*) Miss Marple is referring to Randall Goedler's will.

Craddock Randall Goedler?

Miss Marple He was a financier, Inspector. Very flamboyant. Hailed as a genius in the City.

Miss Blacklock He was. I was his personal secretary—for nearly twenty years. He made millions.

Miss Marple But, without you it might never have happened.

Miss Blacklock You seem very well informed, Miss Marple. Why don't you tell the Inspector?

Miss Marple (*embarrassed*) I'm sorry. I didn't mean to be rude.

A moment passes. Then Miss Blacklock smiles an apology

Miss Blacklock No, I'm sorry, Miss Marple. But, you know that Bunny does get things muddled. You may have got a strange version of the truth.

Craddock What is the *truth?*

Miss Blacklock I loaned Randall Goedler some money in his early days—everything I had. He was up against it—a step from losing all he'd worked for. He didn't. I more or less became a junior partner. When he died he left a fortune.

Craddock To whom?

Miss Blacklock His wife, Belle. In trust for her during her lifetime. When she dies . . . it comes to me.

Craddock gives a long, low whistle

Craddock And you believe this has nothing to do with the shooting?

Miss Blacklock How can it? Rudi Scherz didn't really know me, let alone Randall Goedler. And his will wasn't made public.

Craddock It can be looked up in Somerset House. Tell me, how does Mrs Goedler feel towards you.

Miss Blacklock (*laughing*) I haven't seen her for years we were always great friends.

Miss Marple (*tentatively*) Miss Bunner was saying that her health isn't too good at the moment.

Miss Blacklock Belle was never very strong. But, Randall always said she'd outlive us all—it wouldn't surprise me. The trouble is—well, apparently, she has difficulty remembering anything or anyone now. Poor Belle. I should go and see her. But, she lives in Scotland—and it's such a long way. You know, Inspector, I've had an excellent reason for murdering Belle for years.

Craddock So, if she dies you get everything.

Miss Blacklock Well—most of it.

Craddock (*after a brief moment*) What happens if you die before she does?

There is a pause

Miss Blacklock It goes to Pip and Emma.

Craddock *Who?*

Miss Blacklock (*smiling*) Yes, it does sound funny, doesn't it? Randall had a sister—Sonia. They fell out when she married a man called Dimitri Stamfordis—he sounds Greek, but he wasn't—mid-European or somewhere. A real rogue—very handsome, mind you. Randall hated him.

Craddock So he cut Sonia out of his will?

Miss Blacklock That's quite right, Inspector, but it didn't matter. She was rich in her own right. Anyway. Belle and Randall's lawyers persuaded him to put someone else in the will in case I died before her. Very sensible. Well, the only communication we received from Sonia was a letter to Belle, two or three years after she married, saying Sonia was deliriously happy and had given birth to twins . . .

Miss Marple Pip and Emma.

Miss Blacklock Yes. I suppose the names were some sort of joke between her and her husband. One was born just before midnight and one just after.

Craddock So, there's a young man and a young lady somewhere who stand to become millionaires.

Miss Blacklock If . . . (*She stops herself*)

Craddock If you die before Belle Goedler. Does anyone know what happened to Sonia and her husband?

Miss Blacklock The last we heard they were living in Eastern Europe.

Craddock How old would Pip and Emma be now?

Miss Blacklock Twenty-five or six—something like that.

Craddock They must be found. Have you any idea that they look like?

Miss Blacklock None. There were no photographs—and even if there had been they wouldn't help us to recognize Pip and Emma now.

Miss Marple What did Sonia look like? They may resemble her.

Miss Blacklock Sonia. Oh. She was dark—rather temperamental— and very attractive.

Craddock (*thoughtfully*) Pip—and Emma . . .

Miss Marple Or Sonia, Inspector. Supposing her husband— Dimitri Stamfordis, wasn't it?

Miss Blacklock nods agreement

You said he was a rogue. Supposing he went through all her money. Clearly she'd stand to gain if you died first.

Craddock Dimitri would, too.

Miss Marple Yes.

Craddock So, there are at least four people who would benefit from your death, Miss Blacklock.

Miss Marple Yes.

Miss Blacklock Oh, but you can discount Patrick and Julia now. If I die before Belle Goedler they'll only get a pittance.

Craddock At this stage I don't believe in discounting *anyone*. And I'd advise you to do the same.

The Main Door opens and Mitzi enters pushing the trolley with coffee and biscuits on it. Her darkness is accentuated by the black dress she is wearing. Her petiteness by the flat shoes she has on: and she is a pretty girl

The others turn to her. Mitzi looks at them for a moment, wondering why they are staring at her

Mitzi Is anything wrong?

Miss Blacklock No.
Mitzi Then why you look at me so strange?
Miss Blacklock I hadn't realized. No Mitzi—nothing at all.

Mitzi turns to exit, but Craddock stops her

Craddock Just a minute, Mitzi.
Mitzi What you want, policeman?
Craddock Have you any relations in this country?
Mitzi Why you want to know?
Craddock Any family . . .
Mitzi My family is dead—*massacred.*
Miss Marple I understood they were sent to Siberia.
Mitzi Who told you that?
Miss Marple Miss Bunner . . .
Craddock You mean you have no-one—brother—or something . . .

A moment. Mitzi watches him cautiously

Mitzi I am alone.
Craddock No English relatives? Distant cousins perhaps . . .
Mitzi Me? English? Huh! (*She laughs*) If it was not so funny I would be insulted.
Craddock At some time I'll need to see all your papers . . .
Mitzi (*furiously*) Everything is in order! I report to the immigration authorities every three months . . .
Craddock Calm down. It's routine. I'm obliged to do it.
Mitzi Why you not arrest me now? You think I do this thing—this *murder.* Very well. Arrest me! (*Her hands shoot out, fists clenched*) Put on the handcuffs!

The Main Door opens and Bunny enters, to see Mitzi holding out her hands

Bunny Good! You're arresting her, are you Inspector?
Mitzi I don't care! Arrest me!
Craddock (*irritated*) Put your hands down—I'm not in the mood.

Mitzi puts her hands down

Bunny You should arrest her. She *stole* a cup!
Mitzi I not steal anything, you stupid old woman!
Miss Blacklock (*admonishing*) Mitzi!
Mitzi No. I don't care. She accuses me of stealing. I do not!
Miss Blacklock Bunny, what's it all about?
Bunny One of your favourite coffee cups, Letty. It's missing. They were on the Welsh dresser in the kitchen—and *she* won't let anyone go in there. There were six—now there are only five.
Miss Blacklock I won't be angry, Mitzi. Did you break one?
Mitzi (*her nostrils flaring*) First murder. Now stealing. And why? Because I am a foreigner. That's the truth! (*She raises an accusing finger at Bunny*) It's her. She is the screwy one. She has done something with it and forgotten. She should be put away!

Miss Blacklock You're being very rude, Mitzi. Apologize to Miss Bunner . . .

Mitzi No! I go! You find someone else. I not blacken your doorstep again.

With this Mitzi turns and exits

Miss Blacklock I do apologize for that outburst. Regrettable—but she's always like it.

Craddock I'm afraid she can't leave.

Miss Blacklock Oh, She won't, don't worry. She's such an explosive person.

Bunny And a *liar*! You should check up on her, Inspector. I dare say we'd all be surprised if we knew the *truth* about *her*.

There's a moment's pause

Miss Blacklock (*indicating the trolley*) Well, she does make excellent coffee.

Bunny It's the only thing she doesn't put garlic in.

Miss Blacklock Miss Marple?

Miss Marple I'd love some thank you.

Miss Blacklock Inspector?

Craddock Not right now, if you don't mind. I'd like to take another look round. Perhaps you would show me the rest of the house.

Miss Blacklock Yes, of course. Bunny, you pour the coffee, would you?

Bunny Oh—yes.

Miss Blacklock and Craddock exit

Bunny moves to the trolley to pour out the coffee

You like it black, don't you?

Miss Marple No. I like it white.

Bunny That's right. (*She hands Miss Marple the coffee*)

Miss Marple takes a "sideways" look at it and moves discreetly to the trolley to pour some milk in, and Bunny pours herself a coffee

I don't know how you drink it black. I like mine with lots of milk and sugar. I've always had a sweet tooth.

They both sit down with their coffee

Letty was always teasing me about it when we were children, I remember.

Miss Marple Not many friendships last as long as yours.

Bunny She rescued me, you know.

Miss Marple (*puzzled*) From what?

Bunny I was destitute.

Miss Marple Surely not.

Bunny Don't you believe me?

Miss Marple Oh, yes—of course.

Bunny She's so good. Not only to me—everyone.

Miss Marple She does seem to take rather a lot of people under her wing.

Bunny Too trusting. Too trusting by far.

Miss Marple She doesn't strike me as the sort of person who's easily fooled.

Bunny She's not a woman of the world, you know. Not like us.

Miss Marple But, if she worked for Randall Goedler all those years . . .

Bunny almost drops her coffee, but recovers

Bunny (*flustered*) Oh, yes. She did. Who told you that?

Miss Marple You did. The other day.

Bunny It's a secret. Don't tell anybody. Poor Lotty. Poor poor Lotty. Whenever I think of her that poem comes to mind.

Miss Marple What poem's that?

Bunny (*indignantly*) Why, the one that goes . . . "And sad affliction bravely borne." (*She sighs*)

Miss Marple What "sad affliction", Miss Bunner?

Bunny (*distantly*) I—what?

Miss Marple Sad affliction.

Bunny All those years looking after her sister—only she would have done it.

Miss Marple Tuberculosis, wasn't it?

Bunny Gave up everything—everything. Nobody appreciates her—not like I do. And that Patrick. He's always taking advantage of her.

Miss Marple He seems such a nice young man.

Bunny Huh! He keeps borrowing money from her and never paying it back. It wouldn't surprise me if it was him who put that Rudi Shorts up to coming here last night. Always playing practical jokes. They were probably going to share the proceeds so he could give Lotty the money he owes her. (*She quivers visibly*) He's like all the young people these days. They've no respect—for anything.

Miss Marple Things aren't all that easy for them, you know.

Bunny Come and look at this . . .

Bunny gets up and goes to the sideboard by the wall where the bullets entered. Miss Marple is close on her heels

See what one of them did to this beautiful sideboard. There. A cigarette burn. It's only the young people who smoke in this house.

Miss Marple What a shame.

Bunny Such a beautiful piece.

Miss Marple Yes, so is this. (*She indicates the Dresden figure*)

Bunny Dresden. We have two. A shepherd here. And a shepherdess in the spare room.

Miss Marple No. This is the shepherdess, Miss Bunner.

Bunny Oh! I always thought the shepherd was in this room. Oh, dear, oh dear. This dreadful business, Miss Marple. It really has got on top of me. I'm more confused than ever.

Miss Marple (*noticing the dead violets*) Good gracious. I am sorry, Miss Bunner. The violets have died. I'd hoped they'd stay fresh all through next week.

Bunny How silly of me. I forgot to water them.

Miss Marple But . . .
Bunny No wonder.
Miss Marple Well, never mind. I'll bring you lots more and I think I know
someone who can repair this so you'd never notice it had been damaged.
Bunny That would be wonderful.
Miss Marple I really ought to be going now.
Bunny Must you? It's so nice having someone to talk to who understands.
Miss Marple I have some shopping to do.

Miss Marple moves to the Locked Door but cannot open it

Bunny Oh, no. That one's always sealed up. This table used to be in front
of it. Then people knew they couldn't go through.
Miss Marple Seems like a good idea.
Bunny It was. But, Phillipa suggested it would be better here. She said it
would—integrate—the rooms more. It was two rooms originally, you
see.

*Miss Marple turns back to the door and looks at it more closely. She
notices the hinges have been oiled*

Miss Marple (*thoughtfully*) Is there a key?
Bunny Ah. The builders were very clever. You see, the same key fits all the
locks on the downstairs rooms. So sensible. But there's a different key
for each bedroom.
Miss Marple (*wryly*) So sensible.
Bunny I'll show you.

*Bunny goes to the Main Door and takes the key out of the lock. She returns
to the Locked Door with it and tries to unlock it. It is a little difficult and
Miss Marple steps in to help*

You see—it's very stiff. But you still can't open it.

*Miss Marple however, manages to unlock it without much trouble. It
swings open in absolute silence*

   Miss Blacklock enters through the Main Door

Miss Blacklock (*indignantly*) What are you doing? This door hasn't
been . . .
Miss Marple (*embarrassed*) I—I really am terribly sorry . . .
Miss Blacklock Miss Marple!
Bunny Oh, Letty—it was all my fault. I was explaining to Miss Marple
about Phillipa suggesting you move the table away from the door.
Miss Marple It was my fault, Miss Blacklock. I'm afraid I have an insati-
able curiosity. Please don't blame Miss Bunner. (*She closes the door*) I
really am sorry.
Miss Blacklock No—there's no need. With all that's been going on I'm
afraid I'm a little overwrought.
Miss Marple My nerves are a little on edge too.

Miss Blacklock moves closer to the door

Miss Blacklock This door hasn't been opened since they'd made these two rooms into one. And I believe that was at the end of the last century.

The Main Door opens and Craddock enters, holding a coffee cup

Craddock Ah, Miss Bunner. My Sergeant's found your missing coffee cup. In the bushes by the duck pond.

Bunny How lovely. I should have asked you to find it in the first place, shouldn't I? You being a detective.

Craddock (*wryly*) Yes—it's all part of the job—we find missing budgerigars as well.

Miss Blacklock But, how did my coffee cup get there?

Craddock (*mildly sarcastic*) Using my obvious powers of detection—I would say someone threw it there. (*He smiles at Miss Marple, who is sharing the joke*) Have you any idea why there should be oil in it, Miss Blacklock?

Miss Marple I think I have, Inspector.

Craddock Surprise me, Miss Marple.

Miss Marple The hinges have been oiled—quite recently, I'd say.

Craddock moves to the Locked Door and, after examining it, opens it during the following speech

Craddock What! So that it would open silently. So if Rudi Scherz had an accomplice—it could have been anyone in this room last night. Why should he need to use this door? Well whoever he is, he's the only one who knows the door can be opened, and he may try to use it again. Let's hope I'm here when he does.

The clock chimes the half-hour

Eleven-thirty. I must get back to the station. Would you like a lift, Miss Marple?

Miss Marple Oh thank you. How very kind.

Miss Blacklock Goodness, I haven't fed the ducks yet . . .

Bunny Can I help you, Letty?

Bunny, Craddock and Miss Blacklock move to the Main Door. Miss Marple goes to the sofa to pick up her knitting-bag

Miss Blacklock Well—all right, come along, Poor creatures must be wondering what's gone wrong today. Good-bye, Miss Marple.

Craddock, Miss Blacklock and Bunny exit through the Main Door

Miss Marple picks up the knitting-bag and moves to the Main Door

Mrs Swettenham (*off, calling*) Letty. Letty.

The Locked Door swings open and Mrs Swettenham enters. She has a jar of honey. She moves downstage and stands there.

Miss Marple hears this as she is going out and closing the Main Door

It's me—Clara. I forgot to leave the honey . . .

CURTAIN

ACT II

SCENE 1

The same. The following Sunday afternoon

Miss Blacklock, Patrick, Bunny and Phillipa are in the drawing-room. Miss Blacklock, Patrick and Phillipa are sitting trying to read the Sunday news-papers, but Bunny is sitting twiddling her thumbs, intent on getting their attention: clearly she is feeling sorry for herself

Bunny It was a lovely birthday present, Letty . . .

Miss Blacklock I'm sorry, Bunny. It would have been a better present if I could have got into the shops yesterday.

Bunny No. No. A box of handkerchiefs was just what I wanted. (*But we realize it was not*)

Patrick (*a bit awkwardly*) I'll, er—get you something on Monday, Bunny.

Bunny I don't want you to put yourself to any trouble, Patrick.

Patrick If only the Inspector had let us get away earlier—I really am sorry . . .

Miss Blacklock So am I, Bunny—about the party as well . . .

Phillipa But, we couldn't have gone ahead with it, could we?

Bunny No. That's what I said. I'll have to cancel my birthday party after this dreadful business. I don't mind—it doesn't upset me . . .

Patrick I didn't see why we couldn't have gone ahead with it. I mean, a man none of us knew—came here—tried to rob us and almost killed Aunt Letty—and just because he got what he deserved, you decide poor Bunny has to suffer.

Phillipa I can't believe that even *you* can be so insensitive, Patrick.

Patrick Oh, I'm quite sensitive sometimes—I mean, I have noticed the way you and Edmund Swettenham look at each other.

Phillipa seethes, but tries to control it

Phillipa What's wrong, Patrick? Are you jealous?

Miss Blacklock Whatever's this? Lover's tiff?

Phillipa (*too quickly on the defensive*) It most certainly isn't that!

Patrick (*seizing the opportunity to tease*) Careful, darling. You know what they say about the lady who doth protest too much.

Bunny realizes she has lost her position as the centre of attraction and she cannot allow this situation to continue

Bunny Oh dear, oh dear. Please don't argue. I have such a headache. But what with that dreadful shooting—and all those questions—well, the pain—(*she holds a hand to her head*)—is quite devastating . . .

Miss Blacklock (*a little irritatedly*) Why don't you take something for it?
Bunny No, no—I shall be all right.
Miss Blacklock Don't be silly.
Bunny I can't find my aspirins anywhere, Letty.
Miss Blacklock There's a bottle of aspirin on my bedside table.
Bunny (*weakening*) Thank you—I'm quite capable of withstanding it . . .
Miss Blacklock Of course you are—but, why suffer?
Bunny Well . . .
Miss Blacklock Shall I go?
Bunny No, no, no—the least I can do is get them myself.

*Bunny gets "painfully" to her feet and, making a "great drama" of it
exits through the Main Door*

Phillipa (*to Miss Blacklock*) You really do know her well, don't you?
Miss Blacklock She surprised me this time. Holding out so long before
mentioning her "headache".
Phillipa But you said she'd develop a stinker—and you were right.
Patrick It's a pity we couldn't have the party. She's been looking forward
to it so much.
Miss Blacklock I'm glad it was her suggestion to cancel it.
Patrick I mean—where's the harm . . . ?

There is a pause

Miss Blacklock (*to Phillipa, appealingly*) If we had her cake with tea—and
sort of turned it into a small—party just for the family?
Patrick It'd cheer her up no end. Only a teeny weeny party . . .
Phillipa Oh blast you. You're making me feel dreadful.
Patrick I'll buy you a milk stout down at the One Tun . . .
Phillipa Oh, go away. Well, we've got to have tea anyway. So, why not!
Miss Blacklock Oh, good. Get Julia and tell Mitzi we're going to have the
cake after all.
Patrick Right—oh.

Patrick exits through the Main Door

Miss Blacklock Phillipa. I don't want to be inquisitive—but there's some-
thing worrying you, isn't there?
Phillipa (*after a moment's pause*) Well . . .
Miss Blacklock Is it anything to do with your son?
Phillipa No, he's fine. He loves his school—the fees—well, obviously
they're a bit of a problem . . .
Miss Blacklock Ah—then there is something . . .
Phillipa It'll be all right . . .
Miss Blacklock Anything you tell me will be in the strictest confidence.
Phillipa There's nothing to tell—really.
Miss Blacklock Very well. But, I've got something to tell you that may
help ease your worries.
Phillipa They're nothing I can't cope with.

Miss Blacklock I know you're very independent, Phillipa. I can't help you much at the moment but perhaps soon . . .

Phillipa Please, Letty—don't give it another thought. I shall be able to manage.

Miss Blacklock I want you to know, I spoke to my solicitor yesterday. I'm changing my will. Apart from Bunny's legacy—everything goes to you.

Phillipa is completely taken aback

Phillipa Me? But you can't be serious . . .

Miss Blacklock Oh, yes—it's all in hand.

Phillipa But, I don't want it. You mustn't do this. What about Patrick and Julia?

Miss Blacklock They have no claim on me. You are now the main beneficiary.

Phillipa Why? Why are you telling me all this?

Miss Blacklock Well. I don't think it's at all a bad idea for people to know that I'm changing my will.

Phillipa I can't let you do it . . .

Miss Blacklock Believe me, Phillipa, there's a very good reason for what I'm doing. You won't get much if I die now, but if I live, one day you'll come into a lot of money.

Phillipa Die? You're not going to *die*.

Miss Blacklock You never know.

The main Door opens and Mitzi enters to announce the arrival of Miss Marple, Mrs Swettenham and Edmund Swettenham in her usual stilted manner

Mitzi Here are Miss Marple, Mrs Swettenham and Edmund Swettenham. Thank you, you're welcome.

Mitzi exits

Miss Blacklock gets up to greet the arrivals, who all have little packages

Miss Blacklock Miss Marple, Clara. This *is* a surprise . . . (*Breaking off*) There's nothing wrong, is there?

Mrs Swettenham Wrong?

Miss Marple (*laughingly*) I suppose when the three of us turn up here these days it does seem as if trouble isn't far behind!

Mrs Swettenham (*indignantly*) Well, I certainly hope it is! I've had enough for one week-end!

Miss Marple It's all my fault. Dropping in like this. I called round to Clara and Edmund to suggest it—hope you don't mind. It seemed such a shame. Miss Bunner having to cancel her party.

Mrs Swettenham We thought we'd bring her a little present each. I'm afraid we haven't got anything very exciting.

Miss Blacklock But how kind.

Mrs Swettenham We won't stay, of course.

Miss Blacklock Oh, but you must stay to tea. Mitzi's made a beautiful cake—and Bunny will be so pleased.

Miss Marple We'd love to stay. Thank you.

The Swettenhams and Miss Marple look at one another questioningly. Edmund ventures first

Edmund Yes. Is that all right with you, Phillipa?
Phillipa (*surprised*) Oh—well—yes, of course . . .
Miss Blacklock Good.

Julia and Patrick enter through the Main Door

Julia Well. It looks as if we're going to have a party after all.
Miss Blacklock Well, we won't have the party—just tea.
Mrs Swettenham By the way, Letty. Did you find the honey?
Miss Blacklock Oh, Clara. I am sorry. I forgot. Thank you very much.
Mrs Swettenham I came in the back door and couldn't find you anywhere. How silly of me forgetting to leave it in the first place. We got all the way home before we noticed, didn't we, Edmund?
Edmund (*long-sufferingly*) I'm sure we could have left it until some other time.
Mrs Swettenham But, it was your idea . . .

A moment's pause

Miss Blacklock Actually we did need it. Mitzi always uses honey in her special cake.
Mrs Swettenham (*to Edmund*) You see.

Edmund ignores her and turns to Miss Marple

Edmund Well, Miss Marple, looks like this time you'll be in at the kill.

There is a pause. His tactless attitude is not appreciated

Mrs Swettenham Don't say things like that, Edmund. That's something we all want to forget.
Edmund How can we. It's by no means over.
Phillipa I'm afraid you're right, Edmund.
Mrs Swettenham (*worried*) I'm sure the Inspector is satisfied . . .
Julia I don't think he is.
Patrick He thinks someone paid Rudi Scherz to kill Aunt Letty—and they'll try again.
Miss Blacklock You shouldn't have mentioned that, Patrick.
Edmund Good God. That puts all of us under suspicion.
Miss Marple I'm afraid Inspector Craddock has to include all of us here now.
Patrick Yes. How long were you out in the hall, Miss Marple? We only have your word for it that you were coming up the drive when the shots were fired.

A moment's pause. All eyes are on Miss Marple

Miss Marple My dear boy. I'm sure *I'm very* high on his list.
Phillipa Really? (*In a snide voice*) And you seem to get on so well with him.

Miss Marple I think he finds me mildly amusing . . .

Miss Blacklock (*after a pause, changing the subject*) Patrick, why don't you see if Bunny's coming.

Patrick goes to the Main Door and opens it a chink to look through

Mrs Swettenham Surely there's not going to be any more . . . unpleasantness?

Edmund By that d'you mean any more *murders*, Mother.

Mrs Swettenham Do you have to?

Miss Blacklock Well, I think that it's all over, too. So, let's forget it, shall we? And try to enjoy ourselves.

Patrick closes the door

Patrick She's coming. (*He returns to the others*)

After a moment of waiting, the Main Door opens and Bunny enters. She has the bottle of aspirin in her hand, and is surprised to see them all

All Happy Birthday, Bunny.

Bunny beams like a child, as she goes to them

Bunny But, I cancelled my party.

Miss Blacklock We're all going to have some cake and a cup of tea, Bunny.

Bunny Oh, what a lovely surprise.

Miss Marple hands Bunny a small parcel

Miss Marple And here's a little something to wish you a very happy birthday, Miss Bunner.

Bunny (*taking it*) Thank you. That is kind.

Miss Marple I'm afraid it's only handkerchiefs.

Bunny's face drops

Bunny (*bravely*) Just what I wanted . . .

Edmund hands her a bag

Edmund (*apologetically*) It's only apples from the garden . . .

Bunny's face drops even more

Bunny What a lovely thought . . .

Mrs Swettenham hands her a wrapped jar of honey

Mrs Swettenham And I've brought you some honey . . .

Bunny How kind.

Mrs Swettenham I'm afraid but the bees aren't so very busy just now, so it's only half a jar . . .

Bunny Oh, well—it can't be helped. (*Pause*) I must take these aspirin. I have a thumping headache still . . .

Miss Blacklock Patrick. There's some soda water on the sideboard.

Bunny Aren't I silly having a headache on my birthday.

Patrick goes to the sideboard, takes out a glass and squirts soda into it, then gives the glass to Bunny and replaces the soda water. Bunny takes the glass from him, pops a couple of aspirin in her mouth and swallows them with the aid of the soda water. There is a moment's pause—as all eyes are on her

Miss Blacklock You'll soon feel better.

The Main Door opens and Mitzi enters pushing the trolley. On it is an enormous chocolate cake—Delicious Death. It has one enormous candle in the middle. Ideally, the candle should be lit

Everyone turns as Mitzi pushes the trolley across the room

Miss Marple What a magnificent cake.
Mitzi I excel myself. This time I put a special *secret* ingredient in. Give it that extra bit of *flavour*. Make it *more* than perfect.
Phillipa Have you noticed the candle, Bunny.
Bunny Yes.
Patrick Only *one?*
Miss Marple Of course. There isn't room for all *twenty-one* candles, is there?
Miss Blacklock (*smiling*) You've got to blow out the candle, Bunny.

Bunny steps forward—a picture of happiness. She huffs and puffs before the candle flickers and goes out. They give her a cheer

Phillipa Do hurry up and cut it, Bunny.
Julia Yes, we're all *dying* to try it.

They watch as Bunny picks up the knife and cuts the first piece of cake. She places it on one of the small plates there and offers it

Bunny Who's first?
Miss Marple You! You're the birthday person. You must eat the first slice.
Julia Go on, Bunny. I'll cut the rest.

Julia moves to start cutting the cake into pieces. Bunny starts to nibble on the cake

Miss Blacklock Don't forget to make a wish.

Bunny takes a huge bite and closes her eyes to make a wish. Julia starts to hand the cake around. Everyone takes a piece but does not actually start eating it yet. They are still watching Bunny, who is still wishing

Patrick What are you wishing, Bunny?

Bunny opens her eyes and smiles at him

Bunny I'm not telling. It won't come true.
Julia If I were you, I'd wish him dead.
Patrick If you weren't my sister . . .
Julia (*with an insincere smile*) But I am . . .

Suddenly, Bunny starts coughing. It gets worse and becomes a choking noise

Mrs Swettenham Someone bang her back.

Before anyone can do this Bunny gives a final choke—cheeks puffing and eyes bulging—and drops to the floor.There is a moment, as they all stand there, immobilized; shock and horror beginning to dig into them. Then Miss Blacklock moves to Bunny and the others gather round

Miss Blacklock (*kneeling*) It's the excitement—it's been too much for her . . . (*She undoes the neck of Bunny's blouse*)

Miss Marple joins Miss Blacklock on her knees so that Bunny is between them

Miss Blacklock Someone get some brandy . . .
Phillipa Surely we should call the doctor.
Julia I'll call him. Letty, what's the doctor's number?
Miss Blacklock Five-eight.

Julia is about to telephone this when Miss Marple stops her

Miss Marple (*quickly*) I'm afraid there's no need . . .

All eyes turn to Miss Marple

It's too late.

Patrick, who has been hovering with his piece of cake, looks down at the plate in his hands

Patrick Delicious Death!

CURTAIN

SCENE 2

The same, The following Monday morning

As the CURTAIN *rises Patrick and Julia are alone in the room*

Julia What are we going to do?
Patrick We'll think of something . . .
Julia They're bound to find out—it can't last much longer . . .
Patrick Don't worry . . .
Julia Don't worry? For God's sake, Patrick!
Patrick We'll achieve nothing by panicking.
Julia You will help me, won't you?
Patrick Haven't I—I've done everything you've asked . . .
Julia I know—you've been wonderful.

They kiss

I need you.

Patrick Well, there's no way back. Can't stop now.
Julia What's done is done.
Patrick I did it for you . . .

They kiss momentarily, then break quickly

The Main Door opens and Miss Blacklock and Inspector Craddock enter. She looks worn and tired. Clearly, she feels the loss of Bunny deeply

Craddock Ah. Good morning, Miss Simmons. How are you, Mr Simmons?
Patrick (*warily*) Well—thank you.
Julia Have you found out any more?
Craddock We're making progress—we're not interrupting anything, are we?
Patrick (*a shade too quickly*) Oh, no—nothing at all.
Julia No . . .
Craddock Well . . .
Patrick Oh, I see. We'll go and feed the ducks or something.

Patrick and Julia are about to exit

Craddock Mr Simmons . . .

Patrick and Julia stop, and Patrick turns to Craddock. They are quite close

Patrick (*nervously*) Yes?
Craddock Did you know you've got lipstick on your collar?

Patrick's hand shoots up to his shirt collar. Clearly, he is embarrassed, and Julia is, too. But she makes a better job of hiding her embarrassment

Patrick I—didn't—I mean—I didn't put a clean shirt on this morning . . .
Craddock Well, he can't blame you, can he, Miss Simmons?
Julia Hardly.
Patrick Well—the ducks . . .

They are about to move off

Craddock By the way, Miss Simmons?
Julia Yes?
Craddock You work in the pharmacy at the local hospital, don't you?
Julia (*warily*) That's right.
Craddock Thank you.

Patrick and Julia continue on their way to the Main Door and exit without another word

There are more urgent things. Now, Miss Blacklock.
Miss Blacklock I'm really not up to answering a lot of questions.
Craddock (*sympathetically*) I'll be as brief as I can. But, you've had another lucky escape.
Miss Blacklock I find it more and more difficult to accept your reasoning, Inspector. How can you possibly suggest that I was the intended victim this time? Any one of us could have eaten that cake first.
Craddock I know that . . .

Miss Blacklock And Patrick's suggestion that Clara's honey could have been poisoned is—it's malicious!

Craddock I agree.

Miss Blacklock (*in surprise*) Oh? Then how was the cake poisoned? Did Mitzi——

Craddock (*interrupting*) It wasn't the cake—

Miss Blacklock But . . .

She breaks off, clearly upset. He takes out a bottle of aspirin

Craddock —it was these.

She looks at the bottle of aspirin, amazed

Miss Blacklock My aspirin?

Craddock Exactly. *Your* aspirin. The ones you normally keep by your bed.

Miss Blacklock (*painfully*) No—no . . .

Craddock Someone wants you dead—very, very badly!

A moment's pause. The tension builds

Miss Blacklock I—I'm frightened, Inspector.

Craddock At last! Now perhaps you'll help me find the murderer.

Miss Blacklock (*sharply*) I haven't purposely been non-co-operative. I just couldn't believe anyone would . . . (*She breaks off*)

Craddock There's no friendship where money's concerned. Did you know Belle Goedler's condition has deteriorated recently?

Miss Blacklock I knew she wasn't well . . .

Craddock I understand from the Scottish police that she's now seriously ill.

Miss Blacklock I should go to her. Poor Belle . . .

Craddock It could be poor Miss Blacklock.

She looks at him, afraid

Miss Blacklock Pip and Emma . . .

Craddock Yes. They are uppermost in my mind, but it could be a combination of them and their parents who are trying to kill you. The father. Dimitri Stanfordis. You said he was a rogue. Would he go as far as murder to get money?

A moment's pause

Miss Blacklock (*fearfully*) I'll do anything you say.

Craddock Good. You must try to remember everything you can about him—Sonia—and Pip and Emma. Anything and everything. But, the son and daughter in particular. They're uppermost in my mind. Have you any photographs of them?

Miss Blacklock Well—Belle Goedler is more likely to have photographs of them than I am.

Craddock I'm afraid we drew almost a complete blank with her. They allowed the police up there to look all over the house—they found nothing. Have you anything? What I'm hoping is that Pip may take after his father—or Emma her mother . . .

Miss Blacklock Or the other way round . . .
Craddock Exactly.
Miss Blacklock There was an old album. I haven't seen it for years. It
  should be in the house somewhere . . .
Craddock Find it!
Miss Blacklock It might take a little while.
Craddock Would you like some help?
Miss Blacklock Let me try first! (*Miss Blacklock opens the Main Door*)

*Phillipa is standing there. She enters. Miss Blacklock waits a moment,
then exits, closing the door behind her*

Phillipa I believe you want to see me?
Craddock Yes, Mrs Haymes. Do sit down.

Phillipa sits rather hesitantly

Phillipa Oh, dear—this sounds serious.
Craddock (*after a pause*) If you lie about something, Mrs Haymes—you
  have to cover your tracks very very carefully.
Phillipa I—I don't . . .
Craddock Yes, you do understand. Don't lie any more. You know what
  I'm talking about.

*A moment's pause. During this and the following, Phillipa clenches and un-
clenches her hands*

Phillipa (*bitterly*) Everyone says we have more freedom nowadays—the
  world is—more understanding—than it ever was. Well, Inspector
  Craddock, you try being an unmarried mother . . .
Craddock I don't think it would work!

She smiles in spite of herself

Phillipa It isn't easy in a small village.
Craddock So, you invented a husband!
Phillipa How do you think Letty Blacklock would react if she knew the
  truth?
Craddock She strikes me as being a sympathetic and understanding person. What's more, she's no fool. I've a sneaking suspicion she may have
  guessed the truth.

Phillipa's hand goes up to her mouth

Phillipa So, that's why . . .
Craddock What?
Phillipa She's so kind to me—there aren't many like her.
Craddock Does your son know the truth?
Phillipa He believes—his father died . . .
Craddock Silly. He'll find out sometime.
Phillipa Maybe.
Craddock My advice to you is to tell him—and everyone else.
Phillipa Will you tell the others if I don't? It isn't a crime.

Craddock I couldn't live with it. But, it's up to you.
Phillipa How did you find out.
Craddock We do a lot of routine work.
Phillipa You've been checking up on me?
Craddock Sort of.
Phillipa You make it sound very casual.
Craddock It isn't. But. it *is puzzling*.

A moment's pause

Phillipa Puzzling?
Craddock It's only a small thing—but I'm sure you can help. It's about your son's birth certificate.
Phillipa (*warily*) Yes?
Craddock It gives the mother's name as—Phillipa Haymes.
Phillipa (*nervously*) Well—that's me.
Craddock Ah, well—in that case, there is a problem.

Phillipa drops her head

You see—we can't find a birth certificate—for anyone with your name—well, not one that corresponds with what we know about you.

Phillipa looks up at him and bites her lip

The Main Door opens and Miss Blacklock enters, carrying a photographic album

Miss Blacklock I've found it . . . Am I interrupting?
Craddock Your timing is perfect. Mrs Haymes and I have just finished. (*He pauses*) *For the time being!*

Phillipa gets up, her mind clearly in a whirl, and exits without a word, closing the door behind her

Are there any photos of Sonia and her husband?
Miss Blacklock I haven't had a chance to look yet.

Craddock starts to turn the pages of the album

Craddock (*pointing*) Is that her?
Miss Blacklock No—that's Belle. Isn't she beautiful?
Craddock (*reading*) "Belle at Skeyne"?
Miss Blacklock That's their place in Scotland. I'm afraid the writing is rather faded.
Craddock Tell me when there's one of Sonia and Dimitri. (*He continues to turn the pages and then stops abruptly. He then holds up the album so that we can see two facing pages that are blank. He peers closely at the blank pages. Reading*) "Sonia and Dimitri—Dimitri—Belle, Dimitri and Sonia—Skeyne. Belle, Self and Sonia." (*He stops reading*) Someone got to this ahead of you, Miss Blacklock, didn't they?
Miss Blacklock It looks as though they've been ripped out.

He flicks over a few more pages and then stops, holding up what are clearly some old letters

Craddock Letters.

Miss Blacklock They'll be from me to my sister. (*She holds out her hand to take them*)

Craddock If you've no objection I'd like to skim through these.

Miss Blacklock Well . . .

Craddock (*refusing to be put off*) There might be something—about—Sonia—or Dimitri.

As Craddock mentions the name the Main Door opens and Mitzi enters, with outdoor clothes on, and carrying a suitcase

Mitzi Miss Blacklock . .

Miss Blacklock (*irritatedly*) Please, Mitzi. Not now. I don't want to be interrupted at the moment.

Mitzi I not interrupt! I give you the sack! I go! (*She turns and makes her way back to the Main Door*)

Miss Blacklock Mitzi . . .

Mitzi does not answer. She exits without a backward glance, slamming the door behind her

Miss Blacklock turns to Craddock

(*Appealing*) She can't go . . .

Craddock Certainly not.

Miss Blacklock I'll go after her.

Craddock Of course. And when you catch up with her, you might tell her that she won't get any further than the Bus Station.

Miss Blacklock makes a hurried exit

Craddock sits down and starts to read the letters

After a moment the Main Door opens and Miss Marple enters

Miss Marple Inspector!

Craddock (*covering the letters*) Ah, my little sleuth. You're just in time.

Miss Marple Some people say I'm like a bad penny.

Craddock But, not me, Miss Marple—not me.

Miss Marple I passed Miss Blacklock—she told me to come in. That girl of hers, Mitzi, was haring down the drive like a maniac.

Craddock She is rather peculiar, isn't she? Well. Now you're here you can make yourself useful and help me with a little research. (*He holds up a letter*)

Miss Marple Certainly, but I do have to talk to Miss Blacklock . . .

Craddock It won't take long—and I don't think you'd want to pass up the opportunity of going through someone's old letters!

Miss Marple (*with a broad smile*) Inspector! That's not like me—whose are they!

Craddock holds the letters out to her. She takes them

Craddock It's from Miss Blacklock to her sister, Charlotte. If you find anything that might be helpful—*as well as interesting*—read it out to me, please.

Miss Marple Very well.

They sit down opposite each other and start reading

Craddock Here's something that's been mentioned before.

Miss Marple Oh?

Craddock It refers to her disfigurement—Charlotte's that is. (*Reading*) "It's not as bad as you think it is and you shouldn't lock yourself away . . ."

Miss Marple I wonder what it was—this disfigurement?

Craddock It doesn't say specifically—I don't suppose it was anything much . . .

Miss Marple Then why should she lock herself away?

Craddock In my experience, most women are extremely vain. How would you react if you had a mole on the end of your nose?

Miss Marple I wouldn't have to look at it.

Craddock But, most women would hide themselves behind a veil.

They go back to their respective letters

Miss Marple It's mentioned in this one, too. Listen. (*Reading*) "I do wish you'd get out more. No-one else notices it."

Craddock You see. Pure vanity!

Miss Marple (*thoughtfully*) Maybe.

Craddock (*still looking at his letter*) Ah. This is what I've been looking for.

Miss Marple What is it?

Craddock About Sonia Goedler—the fights she had with her brother. (*Reading*) "Sonia has such a violent temper. It's quite terrifying sometimes."

Miss Marple Did you ever find any photographs of Sonia?

Craddock They've disappeared—rather conveniently. But, violent temper, and Miss Blacklock says she was dark and attractive. Makes you think, doesn't it?

Miss Marple (*thoughtfully*) Yes. It does indeed Inspector. (*She goes back to her letter*) Here's something interesting. (*Reading*) "You can always tell when Sonia is angry. She has the habit of clenching and unclenching her hands." Who does that remind you of?

Craddock You've got me there. That's something I've missed.

Miss Marple And, you don't miss much, do you? Julia Simmons does it when she's—agitated. I've been keeping a very careful watch on that young woman.

Craddock Well, I've checked out both Julia and Patrick Simmons. The French police contacted their mother in the South of France and she confirmed that they were staying here.

Miss Marple Really? There's no mistake?

Craddock Well, unless the woman in the South of France *isn't* their mother.

Miss Marple Could she be Sonia? Keeping out of the way until it's all over.

Craddock The French police must have checked on her. They're very thorough.

Miss Marple So, she is Letty Blacklock's cousin?

Craddock Almost certainly.

Miss Marple I was hoping we'd found Emma—but, I know there was always a possibility I was wrong suspecting Julia. She isn't the only one who does that hand-clenching business. Phillipa Haymes does it as well.

Craddock That's very observant of you, Miss Marple. Ten out of ten.

Miss Marple It's very frustrating that there isn't a photograph of Sonia.

Craddock Yes. Sonia Goedler seems to have disappeared off the face of the earth.

Miss Marple I wonder what this means? (*Reading*) "Lots of love, darling, and buck up. This iodine treatment may make a lot of difference."

Craddock (*thoughtfully*) It must have been some special kind of treatment they used in those days.

Miss Marple For what?

Craddock TB. That is why Miss Blacklock sent her sister to Switzerland.

Miss Marple muses. Craddock moves to the album on the table and starts to flip through. Then he taps the album with his finger

Who does that remind you of?

Miss Marple I must admit, it does look like Clara Swettenham but . . .

Craddock But what?

Miss Marple Well, it is an old photograph, Inspector.

The main door opens and Miss Blacklock enters

Miss Blacklock I'm sorry to keep you waiting, Miss Marple. You wanted to see me?

Miss Marple Yes, please. About the funeral service.

Craddock Well, I must get back to the station. I'll take these with me if you don't mind, Miss Blacklock. I'll return them later. Good-bye, ladies.

Craddock exits

Miss Marple (*as he goes*) Good-bye, Inspector. (*To Miss Blacklock*) I am sorry to disturb you at a time like this. My nephew wanted you to know that he's finalized all the arrangements for the service, but he'd like to know which hymns you'd like.

Miss Blacklock "Lead Kindly Light" was her favourite hymn. Please thank him for me . . . (*She breaks off, grief-stricken*)

Miss Marple is unable to do or say anything for a moment. Then with a supreme effort, Miss Blacklock pulls herself together

I'm sorry—very sorry—forgive me.

Miss Marple Don't. Please don't.

Miss Blacklock It came over me—suddenly—what I've lost. She was my only link with the past. The only one who—remembered. Now she's gone—I'm quite alone—quite alone . . .

Miss Marple I understand. Cousins—nephews—nieces—are all very well.

But when the last person you shared your youth with has gone—then you really are *alone*.

The Main Door opens and Phillipa enters with the morning mail

Phillipa Oh. I'm so sorry.
Miss Marple I'm just leaving.
Phillipa Not on my account, I hope?
Miss Marple No, my dear. There's something I must do. Good-bye, Miss Blacklock.

Miss Blacklock is now completely composed

Miss Blacklock Good-bye, and thank you . . .

Miss Marple exits through the Main Door

Phillipa hands Miss Blacklock a letter

Phillipa Only me and you this morning. Mine's from Harry. He's looking forward to half-term.
Miss Blacklock It seems as though he's only just gone back to school . . .
Phillipa Letty, I—realize it probably isn't the ideal time to mention it, but it is all right, isn't it? Harry coming here for half-term?

Miss Blacklock opens her letter and starts to read. As she does so, the change in her expression is dramatic. From a drained look of weariness to cold, hard anger

Miss Blacklock Phillipa!

Phillipa looks up, noticing the change

Phillipa What's wrong?
Miss Blacklock Where are Patrick and Julia?
Phillipa I—I think they're upstairs. Why?

Miss Blacklock hands Phillipa the letter to read. Phillipa skims through it

I don't understand.
Miss Blacklock (*seething*) Will you please get them for me.

Phillipa nods, hands the letter back and exits through the Main Door, leaving it slightly open

Phillipa (*off*) Julia. Patrick. Letty wants a word with you . . .

We hear a muffled reply. Then Phillipa pops her head round the door

Shall I go?
Miss Blacklock I'd like you to stay.

Phillipa pauses for a moment, then enters, reluctantly. Miss Blacklock is still seething

Patrick enters alone

Patrick Julia won't be a moment.

Miss Blacklock indicates a chair

Miss Blacklock (*sharply*) Sit down!

Patrick is instantly aware that something is wrong

Patrick What is it?

Miss Blacklock I've received this letter. (*Reading*) "Dear Aunt Letty. I hope it will be all right for me to come to you on Tuesday? Patrick was going to let me know but he hasn't. My train arrives at about six-fifteen . . ." (*She stops reading*) It's signed. "Yours affectionately, *Julia.*"

Patrick Oh, God . . .

Miss Blacklock (*indicating the letter*) This is from your sister?

Patrick I'm afraid so.

Miss Blacklock Then who is the young woman upstairs?

Patrick I can explain . . .

Miss Blacklock Do!

Patrick I know it was a stupid thing to do. But, Julia—my *real* sister—didn't want to take up the job at the hospital here. You see, she was offered a job up in the North at some theatre—as an assistant stage manager. She's always been stage-struck and she knew Mother would be furious if she took it . . .

Miss Blacklock Will you please explain who that woman is upstairs?

Patrick I'm trying to. We didn't come straight here when we first came back to England. There were friends to see—parties to go to. That's how we met Julia—the one upstairs, I mean. She and I rather fell for each other and as she wasn't doing anything in particular, it seemed like a marvellous idea for the girls to swop identities. I liked it for obvious reasons. And if Mother believed my sister was here—well, she couldn't object. I was going to tell you but I couldn't in these circumstances.

Miss Blacklock Who is that young woman?

Patrick Well . . .

The Main Door opens and Julia enters

Miss Blacklock turns to face her

Miss Blacklock Who are you?

Julia looks at Patrick. There is a moment's pause

WHO ARE YOU?

Julia I'm Emma Stamfordis.

CURTAIN

SCENE 3

The same. About six p.m., the same day

Craddock is with the "family" group—Julia, Miss Blacklock, Phillipa and Patrick. Julia is sitting directly opposite Craddock, who is making copious notes. The others are seated around

Craddock I'm surprised you decided to stay, Miss Stamfordis.

Julia If I'd tried to make a run for it, you'd only have caught up with me.

Craddock You wouldn't have got out of Chipping Cleghorn.

Julia Are you going to arrest me?

Craddock I would like to know where your brother is first.

Julia I haven't the faintest idea.

Craddock If this is misguided family loyalty . . .

Julia I *honestly* don't know.

Miss Blacklock *Honestly.* I imagine that's a word which doesn't come easily to you.

Julia I know how you must feel about me, but . . .

Craddock (*a tinge angrily*) Perlease. Your *brother*, Miss Stamfordis.

Julia I haven't seen him since we were three years old. When my parents split up it was agreed that I should go with my father and Pip with my mother.

Craddock Let's try something different. Where is your father?

Julia Try the moon! When I was just about old enough to take care of myself—he left me in Istanbul. I worked my way back here.

Craddock Where is your mother, then?

Julia Believe me, I'd love to know that. I've searched everywhere. She made a good job of disappearing. I even went to Scotland to see if I could get some information.

Miss Blacklock You went to see Belle?

Julia Why not? She's my aunt. I also hoped she might help me. But, it was no use. She's not part of this world anymore. Then I got to thinking about my uncle—of course, I knew he was very rich. It occurred to me that if Aunt Belle died, I was probably his only surviving relative. So, I went along to Somerset House and looked up his will. Was I surprised! I searched everywhere for someone who even knew Letty Blacklock. Then I had the most incredible stroke of luck. Through an acquaintance I managed to meet Patrick and his sister. When the swop was suggested I had to stop myself sounding too eager.

Miss Blacklock I admire your self-control. It must have been quite an effort waiting for the right opportunity to take a pot-shot at me.

The telephone rings. Miss Blacklock answers it

Hello, Chipping Cleghorn eight-seven. . . . Hold on. Inspector, it's for you.

Craddock (*into the telephone*) Hello. Craddock here. . . . Yes. . . . What. . . . Well, keep me informed. (*He replaces the receiver*) That's a disturbing development. Miss Marple has been missing since she left here this morning.

A general chorus of exclamations: "*Oh, no*", "*How terrible*", *etc.*

(*Checking his watch*) That's nearly seven hours.

The Main Door opens and Mitzi enters with Mrs Swettenham and Edmund

Mitzi (*unnaturally*) Mrs Swettenham and her son Edmund. Thank you. You're welcome.

Julia has to stifle a laugh

Mrs Swettenham What is it now, Inspector?
Craddock All in good time.
Mrs Swettenham Well, I don't like policemen turning up on my doorstep and asking me to accompany them. My neighbours will be tittle-tattling for weeks.
Edmund I shall be writing to the newspapers about this.
Craddock That'll keep you busy for a change, won't it? (*He turns to Mitzi*) Now, Mitzi. You have something to tell us.
Miss Blacklock Mitzi?
Mitzi Yes. I will tell the whole truth and nothing but the truth. When I first saw what happen on Friday I not do that.
Julia Huh! We all know what a little liar she is!
Craddock *Per-lease!*
Mitzi I am in the dining-room. Like I say. When I hear the gun go off. I look through the keyhole and in the little moonlight—I could see—I could see Miss Blacklock. (*She points at Miss Blacklock*)
Miss Blacklock Me? Oh Mitzi . . .
Edmund That's absurd, she couldn't possibly have seen Miss Blacklock . . .
Craddock Go on, Mr Swettenham. Why stop now? Why? Why couldn't she have seen Miss Blacklock? It was because she saw *you*, wasn't it?
Mrs Swettenham Edmund—that's not possible.
Craddock If Miss Blacklock dies before Belle Goedler two people stand to benefit. Emma Stamfordis . . .
Edmund And you think I'm Pip? That's too fantastic for words.
Craddock Who told you about Pip, Mr Swettenham? I certainly haven't and neither has anyone else in this room.
Phillipa You're wrong, Inspector. I've told him . . .

They all turn to look at her

He isn't Pip! I am.

A moment

You wrongly assumed Pip was a boy. (*To Julia*) Emma, you knew the truth. Why didn't you say so?
Julia Because I suspected who you were. The Inspector was right. I was holding back out of family loyalty. I didn't want to give you away.

Miss Blacklock (*angrily*) You of all people, Phillipa.

Phillipa (*coolly, in control*) I am sorry, Letty. But when my mother died I was desperate for money. Hers had gone years ago. She told me about the will and I discovered for myself that Belle Goedler was seriously ill.

Craddock You *had* gone to a lot of trouble.

Phillipa It was important to me. I wanted security. Not for me, for my son. So, I came here.

Miss Blacklock I was prepared to help both of you.

Phillipa Yes, well—it was part of my plan to get into your good books.

Miss Blacklock (*bitterly*) And it worked, didn't it?

Phillipa But, I grew fond of you.

Miss Blacklock I even changed my will in your favour.

Phillipa That scared me stiff. You said there was a very good reason for doing it. I thought you'd found out who I really was. That you were warning me off from trying to get my uncle's money.

Miss Blacklock (*shaking her head*) You were coming to kill me for it.

Phillipa (*after a moment's pause*) It never occurred to me—even though I felt I was more entitled to it than you. But, there it is. I am Pip. And I'm glad you know. (*She turns her attention to Craddock*)

Craddock You two have been seeing quite a lot of each other, haven't you?

Phillipa Yes. Well, there's no need to suspect Edmund any more, Inspector.

Craddock Isn't there? Mr Swettenham's a struggling young writer—not yet published—who would very much like to marry a rich woman.

Edmund It's not *true*!

Craddock You're in debt up to your eyeballs.

Edmund Nonsense!

Craddock And I can prove it. The bank—the bookmaker . . .

Edmund So what! Does that . . .

Mrs Swettenham (*astonished*) It can't be right—not Edmund . . .

Craddock A rich wife would have solved all your problems wouldn't it? But in order for her to be rich, Miss Blacklock had to die first and you did something about that.

Mrs Swettenham Oh Edmund, no—you couldn't . . .

Craddock Shall we start with your meeting Rudi Scherz in Turin, Mr Swettenham!

Edmund exits quickly through the main door

Phillipa Wait!

Mrs Swettenham Edmund . . .

Patrick Inspector, aren't you . . .

Craddock He won't get far. You'll need to see your solicitor as soon as possible, Mrs Swettenham. I'm sorry about this. I realize it must be a great shock.

Miss Blacklock It seems like a bad dream . . .

Craddock (*to Julia*) I'd like to see you down at the station.

Julia Now?

Craddock It won't take long.

Julia exits through the Main Door

Mr Simmons, would you take Mrs Swettenham home, please?

Patrick Yes. Yes, of course.

Craddock A call to her doctor wouldn't do any harm.

Patrick (*gently*) Come along, Mrs Swettenham . . . (*He takes her arm*) It'll be all right—you see . . .

Craddock Mitzi, you are a magnificent liar.

Mitzi I do well. Yes. I did what you ask?

Craddock To the letter! (*To Miss Blacklock*) Sorry to have given you such a fright.

Miss Blacklock You *are* a clever girl, Mitzi.

Mitzi Thank you, Miss Blacklock. I get you some coffee. You look tired.

Miss Blacklock That would be nice.

Mitzi Black and strong.

Miss Blacklock A little milk if you don't mind . . .

Mitzi Yuk! How you drink it—horrible!

Mitzi exits

Craddock Now, Miss Blacklock, you can relax, you're perfectly safe now

Miss Blacklock Thank God. You might have told me you'd arranged it.

Craddock Then you wouldn't have reacted as you did. It was a little unorthodox, but it worked.

Miss Blacklock What if it hadn't?

Craddock I'd have been in a bit of a mess, wouldn't I?

Miss Blacklock What about Miss Marple?

Craddock Perhaps they've got some news down at the station. I hope to God she didn't find out about Edmund Swettenham before we did.

Miss Blacklock You'll let me know when you hear anything?

Craddock Yes. Of course.

Miss Blacklock If only she hadn't interfered . . .

Craddock I'll see you in the morning.

Miss Blacklock Thank you, Inspector.

Craddock exits as the Main Door opens and Mitzi enters carrying two cups of coffee

Mitzi Here you are, Miss Blacklock. Nice and strong. I put just a little milk in.

Miss Blacklock looks at the coffee and frowns

Miss Blacklock One drop or two?

Mitzi I take a liberty. I do myself some.

Miss Blacklock Of course . . .

They sip their coffee and smile at each other. It is very insincere

Mitzi Now, Miss Blacklock. We have a nice little chat.

Miss Blacklock (*warily*) Oh . . .

Mitzi I need money. Lots of money.
Miss Blacklock (*apparently puzzled*) Why tell me?

Mitzi laughs—a small, cautious laugh

Mitzi I think you will help me.
Miss Blacklock I haven't got any money, Mitzi. None to spare, that is.
Mitzi But, soon—you'll be rich. Very rich. Then you give me lots of money.

There is a moment's pause

Miss Blacklock I, er—don't think I will . . .
Mitzi Oh, yes. You will. Because I help you. Now you help me.
Miss Blacklock But, I pay you to help me—with the cooking—the house . . .
Mitzi No, no, no. That is not what I mean. Just now, I tell a big whopper for the Inspector. Except it isn't a lie. Not this time.
Miss Blacklock You don't know what the truth is, Mitzi.
Mitzi Yes. I think I do. That policeman came to me and say, "Mitzi—you are a good liar". I say—yes, it's true! "You tell lie for me", he say. You say when you look through the keyhole you see—Miss Blacklock in the hall . . ."
Miss Blacklock You did your little bit very well—however, I shan't be paying you for it.
Mitzi Ah. But, he tell me to lie—and it is not a lie. For once—I tell the truth. I did see you in the hall—with a gun in your hand.

Miss Blacklock stands there staring at Mitzi, considering her next move

You give me lots of money. I go to America to see my brother. You never hear from me again.
Miss Blacklock But you haven't got a brother, Mitzi. So, if I give you money you'll probably spend it all and then come back to see if you can get more.
Mitzi (*viciously*) I see you in the hall! You have the gun in your hand. Give me the money or I'll tell the police.

There is a moment's pause

Miss Blacklock (*calmly*) Very well. (*She picks up the telephone*) Here! Phone! Phone the police. Tell them that you saw me in the hall! Tell them that you saw me with the gun. Go on! Tell them! And I'll tell them you're a liar. A liar who's trying to blackmail me.
Mitzi I'm not a liar . . .
Miss Blacklock And you'll be put in prison—like you say you were in your own country.

Miss Blacklock thrusts the telephone in a terrified Mitzi's face and holds it there. There is a moment's pause. Clearly, Mitzi is afraid

I'll tell you why you won't do it. You say you were locked in the dining-room. And you *saw* me in the hall holding a gun. Well, my dishonest

little Mitzi—that is another of your lies. Because the police know and
everybody who was here on Friday night *knows*—that the key was in
the lock. So, it was impossible for you to see anything through the keyhole!

There is a moment's pause. Miss Blacklock is triumphant. Mitzi is terrified

Get out! Get out of here—out of my house—NOW!

Mitzi exits through the Main Door

*Miss Blacklock switches on the Dresden lamp, then closes the window
curtains. The clock chimes the half-hour. She pours herself a brandy and sits.
There is a moment's pause, then Bunny's voice is heard*

Bunny's Voice Lotty. Lotty. It's me, Lotty.

*Miss Blacklock cannot believe her ears. She rises and looks frantically
around the room*

You're in danger, Lotty. Danger . . .
Miss Blacklock Bunny?

*Miss Blacklock is paralysed with fear. She clamps her hands over her ears
but she cannot blot the voice out*

Bunny's Voice Lotty, Lotty.
Miss Blacklock Bunny, dear. I loved you. I really loved you. You meant
so much to me. I didn't want you to die . . .

*The Locked Door opens slightly. Miss Blacklock gasps and moves away
from it. The door swings fully open to reveal a figure standing there*

Miss Marple steps forward

Miss Marple But Bunny had to die. Everyday she was becoming more
and more of a liability.
Miss Blacklock Miss Marple . . . Is this some kind of joke?
Miss Marple I have quite a talent for mimicry, so I'm told.
Miss Blacklock A joke in the worst possible taste.
Miss Marple Such sensitivity doesn't become you, Charlotte.
Miss Blacklock Charlotte is dead. I am Letitia.
Miss Marple Bunny would keep referring to you as Lotty instead of
Letty—at the most inconvenient times. I thought it was a slip of the
tongue—I'm sure other people did, too. But. she was the only one left
who knew the truth—who *remembered*.
Miss Blacklock My dear woman! Bunny always muddled people's names.
Everyone knew it. Mitzi for instance was often called Millie. And at
times she referred to you as Miss Maple. She confused you with the
London store. We were all highly amused.
Miss Marple She was putting you at risk every time she got muddled. You
couldn't take that risk any longer. Any moment she might give it all
away.
Miss Blacklock Miss Marple. How dare you, will you please leave!

Miss Marple moves to the Locked Door as if to exit. She opens it, moves briefly outside but returns after a moment holding a Dresden lamp

Miss Marple Recognize it?

Miss Blacklock It's mine.

Miss Marple And it used to be kept here. (*She moves to the table by the split wall and indicates the other Dresden lamp*) But, this one replaced it. (*She holds out the length of wire attached to the lamp she is holding. We can see that it is very badly frayed*) The flex is frayed. You can actually see the bare wire. Bunny put me on to it when she showed me the "cigarette" burn on the sideboard. She even told all of us at one point that *you* were holding the vase of violets, and *not* the cigarette-box as you insisted.

Miss Blacklock Nonsense! Another of Bunny's muddles. I was handing round the cigarettes. Phillipa will confirm it—she had one.

Miss Marple All eyes were on the clock. As it finished striking you simply emptied the water on to the bare wires—that was the flash Bunny saw —and fused the lights. Very effective.

Miss Blacklock What a vivid imagination you have. I should be careful not to let it run away with you—I imagine your old age pension won't cover solicitor's fees.

Miss Marple I'll risk it.

Miss Blacklock It's your funeral . . .

Miss Marple I plan to live a few more years. When your father died. Your sister *Letitia*——

Miss Blacklock *Charlotte* . . .

Miss Marple —decided to take you to Switzerland.

Miss Blacklock Charlotte had TB. It was the best place for her. I had the money—I loved her dearly.

Miss Marple It was the right decision. You, Charlotte, *were* cured. However, ironically Letty caught pneumonia. And died. You were frantic because with her death the Goedler millions slipped through your fingers. Then it occurred to you. You and Letty had been away from England for years. There were big similarities between you. Why not swop identities with her?

Miss Blacklock My birth certificate. My passport. My bank will confirm that I am Letitia. Oh—and I even have Charlotte's death certificate.

Miss Marple You came back to this country. Dora Bunner heard that Letitia had returned and contacted her because she badly needed help.

Miss Blacklock So. If I was Charlotte then Bunny would have recognized me immediately and any deception I'd planned would have been impossible.

Miss Marple She did recognize you. But, when you explained to her— about Randall Goedler and the will—she actually agreed with you that it was your right to inherit the money and even offered to help you. You were lonely and here was someone who you had always had a great deal of affection for and she could substantiate your deception. You took the risk.

Miss Blacklock Good—very good.

Miss Marple Everything went well for years until a few weeks ago. Then you had some bad luck. You ran into Rudi Scherz. He recognized you as Charlotte. You knew Belle could die at any moment and you knew the sort of man he was. When the news broke that you had inherited the Goedler millions, knowing that you weren't Letitia, there was a strong possibility that he would blackmail you. You dare not allow even the smallest chance of that—you'd never get rid of him.

Miss Blacklock I have my methods of dealing with blackmailers, Miss Marple.

Miss Marple When Rudi Scherz came here to ask for his air fare, it was heaven sent. "Fine," you said, "next Friday is the thirteenth and I'm giving a party for my friends. I want to give them a thrill. You put an announcement in the paper saying a murder is going to take place, here at six-thirty. Then turn up. I'll fuse the lights and you pretend it's a hold up. It'll scare them stiff. Then I'll give you your money."

There is a moment's pause

Miss Blacklock Do go on. It's very interesting . . .

Miss Marple You fused the lights as I explained—went through this door . . .

She goes out through the Locked Door into the hall as she speaks

(*Off*) . . . quickly along the passage, locked Mitzi in the dining-room . . .

She returns through the Main Door, closing it behind her

. . . came back into the room through this door—fired two shots at yourself—except you weren't there . . .

Miss Blacklock How do you account for one of the bullets nicking my ear?

Miss Marple It was too obvious. (*She picks up a pair of scissors from the sofa*) Everyone knows the ear lobe bleeds profusely when cut. A pair of scissors would do the trick. Then you shot Rudi Scherz at point-blank range. (*She puts the scissors down*)

Miss Blacklock I'd laugh—if I didn't feel some pity for you. Feel free to tell Inspector Craddock all you've told me. He'll put it down to the rantings of a senile woman. Because we both know—there's no proof.

Miss Marple Oh?

Miss Blacklock No!

Miss Marple Do you remember Bunny's favourite quotation? "And sad affliction bravely borne." Switzerland is famous not only for curing TB. In a letter to you from Letitia she mentioned "iodine treatment". It baffled me for a while. But, a little research and I discovered that Swiss doctors were famous for perfecting a very special glandular operation—

Without warning Miss Marple steps forward and grabs the three strings of pearls from around Miss Blacklock's neck and rips them off

—for goitre!

Miss Marple's action reveals an ugly and vicious-looking scar which stretches right round Miss Blacklock's throat. Miss Blacklock screams and, during the following, backs slowly towards the scissors on the sofa

I'm perfectly sure when the records are checked, we'll find out that it was Lotty and not Letty who was successfully operated on for a goitre.

Miss Blacklock looks almost insane now. She slowly advances on Miss Marple with the scissors behind her back

What a pity you interfered. You're missing. *Presumed dead.* Edmund Swettenham stabbed you and dumped you in the river . . .

Miss Marple manoeuvres around so that Miss Blacklock now has her back to the Locked Door. Miss Blacklock advances towards Miss Marple

Suddenly both Main and Locked Doors open. Mellors enters through the Main Door, switches on the main lights and remains by the door. Craddock enters through the Locked Door and, in an instant, grabs the scissors from Miss Blacklock and overpowers her

Craddock All right Miss Blacklock. It's all over.

Miss Blacklock (*to Miss Marple*) You interfering . . . There's no need to hold on to me, Inspector . . .

Mellors and Craddock stand on either side of Miss Blacklock. Miss Blacklock moves to the Main Door. Mellors follows

Craddock Are you all right, Miss Marple?

Miss Marple Yes, thank you.

Craddock You did very well.

Craddock moves through the Main Door into the kitchen, calling to the others

(*Off*) All right, everybody. Thank you very much. It's all over.

Mrs Swettenham and Edmund enter through the locked Door

Mrs Swettenham You've no idea what a terrible time I've been through. I shall never forgive you—never.

Edmund I'm sorry, Mother. I could hardly tell you what we were up to. *You* would never have agreed to my doing it.

Julia, Phillipa, Mitzi and Patrick enter through the locked Door

Mrs Swettenham How could you have deceived me like that?

Edmund I said I'd help the Inspector on the condition that I'd be the first to get all the facts. I'm convinced somewhere in all this there is a fascinating novel to be written and if I don't write it, someone else will.

Julia What does the Inspector want with us now?

Phillipa He didn't say.

Mitzi The Inspector—tell me to come in' here and bring these. Hey—what you think of my acting—uh?

Patrick (*sarcastically*) Were you acting, Mitzi?

Mitzi I was even better when I pretended to blackmail Miss Blacklock. I give up cooking—and go on the stage.

Craddock enters through the Locked Door

Craddock I owe you an apology, Mrs Swettenham. I really am sorry but the fewer the people who knew what I was up to—the better. (*To Phillipa*) That's why I couldn't tell you, either.

Phillipa Supposing I hadn't come to Edmund's rescue and admitted to being Pip?

Craddock There was no real danger of that, was there? Well—now you're all here—I've got a little surprise for you. (*He moves into the hallway and fetches the chocolate cake from outside*) I thought you'd all be in the mood to enjoy it now. Delicious Death! It's already cut—so dig in! (*He offers the cake to everyone*)

No-one seems enthusiastic

Mrs Swettenham?

Mrs Swettenham No thank you. I'm on a diet.

Craddock Per-lease . . .

Miss Marple rises from the chair and at the same time, both she and Craddock take a large slice of cake each. They look at everybody else and then back to each other

Craddock Funny people!

With this Miss Marple and Craddock each take a gigantic bite from their pieces of cake, as—

the CURTAIN *falls*

FURNITURE AND PROPERTY LIST

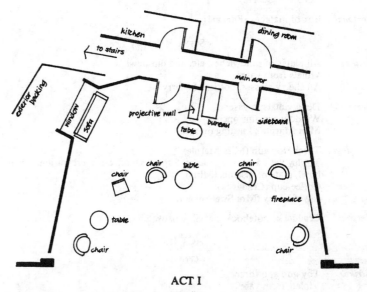

ACT I

SCENE 1

On stage: "Craftsman's" occasional table. *On it:* Dresden shepherdess lamp, silver cigarette-box

Sheraton bureau. *On top:* Art Nouveau china vase

Sideboard. *On it:* tray with various drinks, including sherry, brandy, soda water; assorted glasses; flower vase

2 small occasional tables. *On one:* telephone 6 or 7 small chairs of different styles. *On two:* newspapers

Sofa (in window bay). *On it:* cushions

On mantelpiece: French Empire clock

On walls: various paintings, framed silhouettes

Window curtains—net and velvet

Key in Main Door

Carpet

Off stage: 2 copies of *Chipping Cleghorn Gazette* **(Patrick, Mitzi)**
Bunch of violets in tissue paper **(Miss Marple)**

Personal: **Miss Blacklock:** strings of pearls

SCENE 2

Strike: Newspapers

Set: Plates of sandwiches, cheesy biscuits, dip-bowl, on small centre table
Loose cigarettes beside cigarette-box

Off stage: Bottle of sherry **(Patrick)**
               Flashlight **(Scherz)**
               Revolver **(Scherz)**

Personal: Box of matches **(Edmund)**

SCENE 3

Strike: All plates of sandwiches, etc. and dip-bowl
               Violets from vase
               All sherry glasses, bottles of sherry

Set: Dead violets in vase
               Window curtains open
               Miss Marple's knitting on sofa

Off stage: Torch, toy gun **(Miss Marple)**
               Trolley with 5 cups, 5 saucers, 5 spoons, coffee-jug cream-jug, sugar-
               bowl, plate of biscuits **(Mitzi)**
               Coffee-cup **(Craddock)**
               Jar of honey **(Mrs Swettenham)**

Personal: **Craddock:** notebook, pencil, wristwatch

ACT II
SCENE 1

Strike: Toy gun and torch
               Violets from vase
               Trolley and coffee-cups

Set: 3 Sunday newspapers on chairs

Off stage: Wrapped package of handkerchiefs **(Miss Marple)**
               Bag of apples **(Edmund)**
               Wrapped half-jar of honey **(Mrs Swettenham)**
               Bottle of aspirin **(Bunny)**
               Trolly with chocolate cake, candle in centre, cake knife, 8 small plates
               (Mitzi)

SCENE 2

Strike: Dirty glasses, etc.
               Newspaper
               Aspirin
               Presents
               Trolley and plates

Off stage: Bottle of aspirin, from Scene 1 **(Craddock)**
               Photograph album with loose letters and card **(Miss Blacklock)**
               Suitcase **(Mitzi)**
               2 letters, 1 sealed, 1 open **(Phillipa)**

SCENE 3

Set: Sewing-bag with scissors readily available on sofa

Off stage: 2 cups of coffee **(Mitzi)**
               Dresden shepherd lamp with frayed flex **(Miss Marple)**
               Chocolate cake, from Act II Scene 1 **(Craddock)**

LIGHTING PLOT

Property fittings required: chandelier, wall brackets, 2 Dresden lamps (only 1 practical)

Interior.   A drawing-room. The same scene throughout

ACT I, SCENE 1.   Day
To open: General effect of late autumn morning light
No cues

ACT I, SCENE 2.   Evening
To open: General effect of late October afternoon light

Cue 1	**Miss Blacklock** turns on main lights	(Page 12)
	Snap on chandelier and wall brackets	
Cue 2	As clock finishes chiming	(Page 18)
	Black-out	
Cue 3	**Miss Blacklock**: "There's no need . . ."	(Page 19)
	Snap on chandelier and wall brackets	

ACT I, SCENE 3.   Day
To open: As opening of Act I, Scene 1
No cues

ACT II, SCENE 1.   Day
To open: General effect of early afternoon autumn light
No cues

ACT II, SCENE 2.   Day
To open: As opening of Act I, Scene 1
No cues

ACT II, SCENE 3.   Evening

Cue 4	**As CURTAIN rises**	(Page 55)
	Start slow fade to dusk	
Cue 5	**Miss Blacklock** switches on Dresden lamp and closes curtains	(Page 60)
	Snap on lamp spots; reduce overall lighting as curtains close	
Cue 6	**Mellors** switches on main lights	(Page 63)
	Snap on full interior lighting	

EFFECTS PLOT

ACT I

SCENE 1

No cues

SCENE 2

Cue 1	**Phillipa:** "Thank you, Edmund." *Clock chimes half-hour*	(Page 18)
Cue 2	**Scherz:** "Now!" *Three revolver shots*	(Page 18)

SCENE 3

No cues

ACT II

SCENE 1

No cues

SCENE 2

No cues

SCENE 3

Cue 3	**Miss Blacklock:** "... take a pot-shot at me." *Telephone rings*	(Page 55)
Cue 4	**Miss Blacklock** closes the curtains *Clock chimes half-hour*	(Page 60)

MADE AND PRINTED IN GREAT BRITAIN BY
LATIMER TREND & COMPANY LTD PLYMOUTH

MADE IN ENGLAND